FAITH

A Folly Beach Christmas Mystery

BILL NOEL

ENIGMA HOUSE PRESS

ISBN: 978-1-948374-34-7

Enigma House Press

Goshen, Kentucky

www.enigmahousepress.com

FAITH

Chapter One

The Folly Beach Christmas Parade is one of my favorite events of the year. Not only does it pay homage to the celebration that has a magical way of touching most of us on several levels, but it also gives my fellow residents an opportunity to show, no, to shout, their unique, quirky take on the holiday. Marching bagpipers sharing the same street with shiny waste-removal trucks, and golf carts overflowing with colorfully dressed elves. Add a UPS truck driver wearing a giant Santa's hat, city officials and other bigwigs chauffeured in vintage convertibles, riders dressed as reindeer riding yellow mopeds, and since Folly Beach, South Carolina, is not known as the snow capital of the country, a vehicle filling the air with artificial snow. Not a glimmer of beige interrupted the colorful feast for the eyes. Today was festive for children of all ages, for adults who want to relive their days of youth, and for those who simply love to see smiles. Count me among the latter group.

Today was perfect. It was approaching mid-December,

yet the temperature was hovering in the tolerable sixties, the sky a crisp blue, with the unfiltered sun reflecting off every shiny surface. My friend Charles Fowler and I were watching the festivities from the ninth-floor walkway of the Tides Hotel, Folly's tallest building. We had a perfect, unobstructed view of the parade as it made its way four short blocks up Center Street, appropriately named since it roughly bisected the small, barrier island plus being its center of commerce. The crowd lining both sides of the street was treated to the festivities. Most of the children were waiting for the arrival of Santa, perched on one of Folly's fire engines instead of riding in a reindeer-propelled sleigh, while their parents reveled in laughing at or laughing with many of the parade participants. Charles and I were in the later stages of our sixties, so we didn't have young children to be sharing the sights and sounds with. We stood along the walkway's railing savoring the enjoyment of others.

The fire apparatus carrying the man most youngsters had come to see turned on Center Street when it stopped. Two firefighters jumped from the rig then moved to the rear of the vehicle while yelling something to Santa's helper. At the same time, the sound of laughter from paradegoers was interspersed with the high-pitched sirens of two police vehicles. A second fire engine pulled out of the combination City Hall and Department of Public Safety, a block from the parade's starting point. Police officers on foot stopped the parade to allow the emergency vehicles to cross the line of the parade. Onlookers scampered out of the way of the emergency vehicles as they crossed Center Street then sped up East Cooper Avenue, perpendicular to the parade route.

Santa was escorted off the fire engine as his handlers commandeered a golf cart holding two colorfully attired elves. The fire apparatus then backed up to turn east on Ashley Avenue, Folly's longest street.

Charles pointed to the police and fire vehicles moving away from the center of town. "Unless they're heading to another parade, something big is going on," he said, sharing one of his rare understatements.

A second parade was a nonstarter, but evicting Santa told me the emergency vehicles weren't responding to a cat stuck in a tree. A glance to the east reinforced my suspicion. Approximately four blocks east of Center Street billowing black smoke invaded the blue sky. From our elevated vantage point, I saw reddish-orange flames under the plume of smoke.

Before I pointed it out to Charles, he grabbed my shoulder, pushed me the direction of the elevator, and said, "Let's go."

I followed without needing convincing. What did take time was the wait for the elevator. It wasn't an eternity but seemed like it before the doors opened. Sure, we could've gone down the stairs, but don't forget our age. We weren't fit enough to traipse to ground level.

Center Street was lined with people enjoying the parade oblivious to what was happening a few blocks away. We weaved through the mass of people clogging the sidewalk along Center Street so we could follow the path Santa's former ride took. The fire was at least three blocks past my cottage on the other side of Bert's Market. Two engines from nearby James Island screamed past us. A few spectators from the parade had made their way the direction we were headed. Fires trump a parade almost every time.

I couldn't see what was burning but didn't doubt it was big. A couple of two-story apartment buildings were on East

Ashley. From the number of emergency vehicles plus the amount of smoke filling the sky, I'd wager one of them was the subject of so much attention. The road was blocked two streets in front of us. Traffic was backed up from where it was being rerouted off Ashley. I was glad we were walking rather than stuck in the line of stopped vehicles.

We passed the first apartment building realizing the fire was in the other structure. Another fire truck pulled up behind us, siren blaring, with the added sounds of its horn attempting to get the stuck traffic to pull over so it could pass. It was having little success.

Charles tapped the handmade wooden cane he carries for no apparent reason on the pavement like it would give him extra speed. I slowed to catch my breath. The closer we got, the smell of burning wood, ashes floating in the air like leaves from a tree on a windy fall day, combined with shouts from firefighters, indicated little would be left from the burning structure still blocked from our view by two houses.

Allen Spencer, an officer with the Folly Beach Department of Public Safety I'd met when I first moved to Folly more than a decade ago, was in front of his patrol car which was diagonally parked blocking traffic. He was furiously waving his arms to get vehicles to turn off East Ashley. When I met Allen, he was new to the department, young, trim, and moved with the grace of a surfer, which he was. Since then, he'd gained thirty pounds. While still dedicated to work, he'd acquired the cynicism adopted by many law enforcement officials after years on the job. He considered me a friend, so he shared more than he would with most civilians.

We stopped beside Allen's patrol car where we got our first look at what was burning. The fire was, as I'd figured, in the two-story apartment building. The aging, wood-frame, six-unit structure was fully engulfed. Most of the roof had collapsed. Even though several hoses spewed water at the building, flames were still reaching out from the windows on two of the three first-floor apartments. The stairs to the second-floor walkway were barely attached to the building, appearing ready to collapse. It wouldn't have mattered since the walkway across the front of the building leading to the apartment doors had already fallen. Allen nodded in our direction but was too busy to tell us what he knew about the fire. We passed two Ford pickup trucks, a high-end SUV, and a Harley Davidson parked adjacent to the apartment's parking lot. Ashes rained from the sky like large, black, sinister snowflakes dotting the top of the vehicles.

Two ambulances from Charleston, seven miles from Folly, pulled up to Allen's car. He scurried to move it so the emergency vehicles could join the large gathering of first-responder vehicles. My first thought was that if anyone was in the building during the fire, ambulances would probably not be needed.

The building was a total loss, my prayer was that no residents were.

Chapter Two

Yellow police tape was strung fifty yards each direction from the burning structure. The group of bystanders, increasing by the minute, edged close to the barrier. Many of those gathered, Charles and I included, were startled when the remaining section of the roof collapsed. Smoke rolled toward us as fingers of flames darted from around the fallen roof. It may've startled us, but it didn't stop two couples from inching closer to the building, pushing the crime scene tape out of the way as they moved toward the fire.

Trula Bishop, another police officer I'd known since she moved to Folly four years ago, glared at the intruders. She yelled for them to move back as she rushed across the gravel lot to confront the trespassers. Fortunately, they obeyed. Trula saw Charles and me standing obediently behind the tape, then snarled at the offenders before coming over to us.

"Mr. Chris, Mr. Charles, should've known you'd be here.

Something bad happens, you magically appear." She shook her head.

Trula was a double minority in the Folly Beach Department of Public Safety. She was one of the few women wearing a badge and even more in the minority being African American. Like most of Folly's first responders, Trula lived off-island. I knew little about her personal life but knew she was good at her job. Over the years, she'd helped me out of a couple of scrapes I'd gotten in while, along with a few of my friends, helping bring some serious criminals to justice.

That wouldn't have been unusual if my background had been in law enforcement. It was more than unusual since my entire working career was as a human resource professional with a large healthcare company in Kentucky. The closest I'd come to law enforcement or criminals before retiring to Folly was watching TV cop shows. Some cosmic switch was thrown when I crossed the Folly River the first time. My first week here, I stumbled on a murder victim as I was photographing the iconic Morris Island Lighthouse, visible from the east end of Folly. The murderer figured I may've seen him, which I hadn't by the way. His solution for silencing me was to do it permanently. I'm still around, so he clearly failed, but not by much. Oh well, that's a story for another time. In the years since that fateful encounter, I, along with some friends, had helped the police solve a few murders, murders that had either touched me or my close acquaintances. That's how Officer Bishop and I'd become acquainted.

I ignored her comment. "Trula, we were watching the Christmas parade from the Tides when—"

"When the jolly old man was dumped off the fire

engine," Charles interrupted. "Chris said we'd better get nosy. So, here we are."

Not exactly how I remembered it, but it'd be a waste of words correcting him.

I said, "Trula, what happened?"

Charles interrupted, "Think someone was roasting chestnuts on an open fire and it got out of control?"

Trula stared at him.

"You know," Charles said, "Like in 'The Christmas Song'?"

The officer shook her head then glanced at the building, or what was left of it. Flames had died down, but black smoke still filled the air. "Chris, I don't know. It was fully engulfed when we arrived. I doubt there was anything we could've done to save it."

I followed her gaze, the one she gave after ignoring Charles's question. "Anyone in there when it started?"

"Our guys got a quick look in the three apartments on the first floor before the roof started falling. They didn't see anyone. The front walkway up there was already about to fall before we could get to the second floor. I hope no one was up there. If they were, well…."

"Any idea what started it?" Charles said.

Trula shook her head. "The building's old, wood, a fire waiting to happen. With that said, it went up fast, too fast."

I said, "Arson?"

"Mr. Chris, I'm no expert, but it wouldn't surprise me. If she hasn't already, The Chief will call in the Charleston Fire Department Fire Marshall Division. They're the experts. If it was arson, they'll figure it out. Fellas, I need to get back to playing cop."

"One more question," I said. "Do you know if any of the people standing around lived there?"

Trula looked at me with a slight smile. "Giving up your career as a private detective to become a fire investigator?"

I smiled. "Charles is the private detective. I'm the old, retired bureaucrat."

Years earlier, Charles self-proclaimed he was a private detective. He'd never studied to be a detective, nor had he ever worked under a licensed pro, a requirement in South Carolina. What he'd done, or claimed to have done, was read every novel in print featuring private detectives.

Charles beamed, apparently because I'd acknowledged his self-imposed status. Note to self, make sarcastic remarks more apparent.

Charles said, "Don't worry, Officer Bishop, I'll remain a private detective, and my friend Chris will still be old."

Trula sighed. "Over with Chief LaMond. The woman with the boy."

Charles said, "Huh?"

"Mr. Charles, pay attention," Trula said. "Chris asked if anyone hanging around lived in the building."

"The woman with the kid lived there?"

"Mr. Charles, you are a detective after all."

Trula was better at sarcasm than I.

I said, "Who are they?"

Before she answered, the steps to the second floor pulled loose and crumbled to the ground stirring a cloud of dust. The smoke that bellowed moments earlier, was barely visible. A couple of firefighters were moving into the lower apartments, or what was left of them. I doubted they'd find anything usable. One of the ambulances was turning to start its trip back to Charleston. The good news was it would be returning without anyone needing medical attention.

"Yeah, who?" Charles added as if my asking wasn't enough.

Trula grinned. "Mr. Charles, I thought you knew everyone over here."

"Only everyone with pets," he said.

That wasn't much of an exaggeration.

"The woman is Rosalynn Wheeler, goes by Rose. Her son's Luke."

The woman Trula referred to appeared in her mid-forties, about five-foot-five, average weight, with curly brown hair. Luke was nine or ten, although I'm not good at guessing ages. He was chubby and looked at the ground and not at his mother as she talked to Chief Cindy LaMond.

I'd known Chief LaMond since she arrived on Folly a year after I retired to the island. She moved up the ranks quickly, was named Chief three years ago.

"Does her name ring a bell?" Trula added.

"No," Charles said.

I shook my head.

"Wow, Mr. Charles. I know something such an outstanding private detective as yourself doesn't know."

"What would that be, Trula?"

"She's your Police Chief's sister."

Chapter Three

Cindy LaMond and I'd been friends going on a decade, but I knew little about her life before she arrived on Folly. She grew up near Knoxville, Tennessee, had worked for a Sheriff's Office before coming here, yet beyond that, not much. I didn't know she had a sibling.

I said, "Sister?"

"Don't feel bad, Cindy is my boss, I've worked closely with her, almost daily, for four years. I didn't know anything about a sister until she brought her by the station two weeks ago to introduce her."

"When did she get here?" I asked.

"Miss Rose arrived a few days before the Chief introduced us."

Charles said, "What else do you know about her?"

"Next to nothing. I'd guess she's recently divorced."

Charles glanced at Cindy, her sister, and Luke, then turned to Trula. "Did she say that?"

"No. Her ring finger has a white band of flesh where a wedding ring would go."

"She have pets?" Charles asked, as only he would.

Trula grinned. "Does a son count as a pet?"

"So, no pets?" Charles said.

Trula sighed. "None I'm aware of."

The fire appeared under control. Two James Island fire vehicles weaved their way out of the lot in front of the cremated building before pulling back on Ashley Avenue. Cindy, her sister, and Luke were moving out of the trucks' way when Cindy spotted us. She rolled her eyes, put her arm around her sister, then escorted her relatives our way.

"Chief," Trula said, "I caught these vagrants hanging around. Figured they were up to no good. Want me to arrest them?"

Cindy smiled. "Good police work, Officer Bishop. Tell you what, why don't you help Officer Spencer herd that line of traffic off Ashley. I'll take care of these troublemakers."

Cindy watched Trula leave, then turned toward Charles and me. "Guys, let me introduce you to Rosalynn Wheeler and her son Luke."

Rosalynn was two inches taller than Cindy. She shared Cindy's endearing smile, when she said, "Please call me Rose. It's nice to meet you. Cindy tells me you're a couple of her friends."

I said, "I'm honored to say that's true."

"We're a couple of her favorite citizens," Charles said, not to be left out.

Cindy tapped his arm. "That's compared to criminals, slimeballs, other assorted deviants I deal with."

Time to move along. "Rosalynn, ummm, Rose, Officer

Bishop told us you lived there." I nodded toward the smoldering pile of wood.

"Yes, we moved here three weeks ago and found an apartment there until we decide if we want to buy or rent."

Charles asked, "Where'd you move from?"

"Morristown, Tennessee. It's a small town northeast of Knoxville."

"What brings you to Folly?" Charles asked, never fearing to tread on personal ground.

Cindy stepped between Charles and Rose. "Guys, as you can see, no one will be returning to that building anytime soon, correction, anytime at all. They'll stay with Larry and me until they make other arrangements." She pointed to a row of vehicles in the parking lot. "That's Rose's Ford Explorer blocked by our fire apparatus, so it'll probably be a couple of hours before it can leave. Got a favor to ask. Could you walk Rose and Luke to my house so they can start settling in?"

"Cindy," Rose said, "I can find my way. I don't need an escort."

"Rose, I'd feel more comfortable if you'd let them go with you."

"It's no problem," I said. "I'd be glad to walk you and Luke. Cindy, does Larry know they're coming?"

Larry and Cindy had been married eight years and lived in a house on East Indian Avenue. While only six or so blocks from here, it's not a straight shot.

"Chris, you know hubby keeps himself handcuffed to the cash register this time of year. It's his big season. He's the only person I know who gets excited about someone buying a plunger to unclog a toilet. I'll be home long before he gets there and realizes we have boarders."

In addition to being married to Cindy, Larry owns Pewter Hardware, Folly's tiny hardware store.

I turned to Rose, "Ready to go?"

"Let me grab something out of my vehicle."

I nodded.

She walked to the Explorer with Luke matching her step for step.

Cindy watched them step over the firehoses snaked across the parking area, then said, "Chris, she's ten years younger than me, so I missed out on much of her life. I was already out of the house, moved out of our tiny hometown of Kodak, Tennessee, was working at various dead-end jobs in Knoxville during her junior-high and high-school years. The main thing I know is that she's by far the smarter chick of the two of us."

"Cindy, that's going some. You're as smart as most people I know."

"Yeah, maybe, but look who you're comparing me to." She pointed to Charles.

I laughed.

Charles said, "Chief, that makes you a genius."

That got a chuckle out of Cindy before she turned serious. "Don't know all the circumstances why she surprised me by showing up. I know she's fragile. Don't think it'd take much to break her from holding it together. I'd guess the only thing holding her together now is knowing she has to for Luke."

Charles kept an eye on Rose, yet said to Cindy, "You and Larry have a big house. How come they didn't move in with you until they found somewhere to live?"

"Excellent question, Charles. I asked the same thing. She said there was no way she was going to interrupt Larry and my way of life, whatever the hell that meant. Suppose that's going to change now."

Rose and Luke returned. She carried a small box. From the logo on it, I'd guess it held a new cell phone.

I didn't have to guess, when she said, "Got a new phone yesterday. My old one does everything well except make phone calls. The guy at the store said it'd cost more to fix than to replace. Fortunately, I hadn't gotten it out of the SUV. If I had, it'd be, well, you can see what it would've been." She nodded toward the apartment.

Cindy handed Rose a key to her house, then Charles said, "Chris, go on and escort Rose and Luke. I'll stay to talk to some of the folks gawking at the smoldering rubble."

Translating Charles speak, that meant he wanted to nose into whatever happened; nose into things that were none of his business.

Chapter Four

We were a block from the apartment building before the air stopped smelling like burning wood, but we could still hear firefighters wrapping up.

Luke kept looking back at the frightening scene, before saying, "Mom, everything we have is gone. What're we going to do?"

Rose reached for his hand. He yanked it back. I didn't know if he was being a typical nine-year-old not wanting to show affection in front of a stranger, or something deeper.

She smiled. "Luke, you're right, our stuff is gone. Tell you what, let's look at it like an adventure. We'll get new things. Everything will be okay."

I was impressed with her attitude. I hoped she was sincere, not simply putting on a positive front for Luke.

"Mom, that's the same thing you said when we left home. Maybe we should go back to Tennessee where everything was okay." His voice broke, he hesitated, then said, "We had a house, we had stuff, we had friends. Mom, we had dad."

Rose's hand shook as she put it around Luke's shoulder. This time he didn't pull away. I didn't want to intrude on their personal moment, so I took a couple of strides ahead of them, then continued to Cindy's house.

The festivities on Center Street must've ended. Several groups of people passed us going the other direction, most laughing and enjoying the day with exceptional December weather. Then I saw a familiar face.

Dude Sloan was humming "Rudolph the Red-Nosed Reindeer," while skipping, yes, skipping, down the middle of the street followed by his Australian Terrier Pluto hooked to a rhinestone-studded leash. Dude would've been hard to miss in his white T-shirt with a large DayGlo red and green peace symbol on the front. Dude, real first name James, was a longtime resident of Folly, owner of the surf shop, looked like a five-foot-seven version of a cross between Willie Nelson and Arlo Guthrie, was in his mid-sixties, and comfortable living like an aging hippie stuck in the 1960s. Pluto looked like a shorter version of Dude. I was privileged to count Dude as a friend.

"Yo, Chrisster, Merry Christmas Parade. Got new family?"

Did I fail to mention Dude's vocabulary and speech pattern are challenging to say the least? That's appropriate since Dude's specialty is saying the least.

The first spark of life I'd seen in Luke was when he left his mom's side, then bent to rub Pluto's chin.

"What's his name?" asked the young man who appeared

to have gotten over worrying about his future. He'd found a new friend.

"Pluto," Dude said. "Be named for dwarf planet. You be?"

Luke stood, shook Dude's hand, and said in a full, confident voice, "Luke Wheeler, pleased to meet you, Mr. Dude."

"No mister, just Dude."

"Dude," I said, "Luke is Chief LaMond's nephew. This is Rosalynn, Luke's mom."

"Woe, Dude not great at family branches. That make you Chieftress's sis?"

"Yes. Please call me Rose."

"Your sis be great gal. Nephew Luke be polite. Rare in youngins. Be visitin'?"

Rose smiled. "No, we've moved here from Tennessee."

"Cool. Rocky Top state," Dude said as Luke turned all his attention back to Pluto. "Where be livin'?"

Rose shook her head. "We were living in the apartment building that had the fire. Now we're heading to my sister's house until we find somewhere to relocate."

"Woe," Dude said for a second time. "You be in building that be giant weenie roast? You okay?"

"We're fine. Thanks for asking."

"Pluto plus me be at holiday parade, heard sirens like there be convention of fire folks. Someone said, Ashley Avenue apartment building gone. Glad you be okey dokey."

That was a long speech for Dude, so I told him we'd better be heading to Cindy's house.

"Cool. Be needin' anything. Clothes, surfboards, pup to hug, I be at surf shop. Don't be stranger."

Rose thanked him as he continued skipping to wherever.

"Interesting man," Rose said.

That was like calling an octopus an interesting looking creature.

"Mom, do we need a surfboard?"

"Think we need to get to Aunt Cindy's first, then get some clothes, food, then—"

"Got it," Luke said as he rolled his eyes.

"Rose," I said, "were you at the apartment when the fire started?"

"No, I was in Bert's Market yesterday when someone told me about the parade. Thought it'd be fun for Luke. We were standing by Snapper Jack's watching the festivities when I heard sirens. I didn't think much of it. I figured there'd be fire engines and police cars in the parade. They use their sirens when they're in the parades I've attended. Then more sirens, so I looked down Ashley toward our apartment. That's when I saw a fire truck heading toward the building. Luke pointed out the smoke. I didn't know what was burning but could tell it was near our place. We headed home to see for sure. You know the rest."

"That had to be terrifying."

"Not nearly as bad as it would've been if we were in the apartment."

"What floor were you on?"

"First, the unit nearest the street."

"Had you lived there long enough to meet other residents?"

"Not really. The middle unit, the one next to ours, was vacant, had been for five months, I'd heard. A man lived in the far unit, but I never met him. Upstairs there were two women, or that's what the landlord said, and a young man.

He introduced himself to me the day I moved in. Think his name was Ty, didn't catch his last name. Sorry, that's all I know."

"Ty Striker?"

"Could be. Who's he?"

"Works at Bert's. He's the only Ty I know. Describe him?"

"Early twenties, tall, maybe six-foot-one, thin, face not yet out of the acne years. He was friendly, smiled a lot. Sorry, I don't know anything else."

"That's okay. I was curious."

"The landlord could give you the names."

"What's his name?"

"Russell O'Leary. I can give you his number. I don't think he lives on Folly."

Luke listened to our conversation, then interrupted. "Mr. Landrum, does that Dude man surf? He looks old for a surfer."

I laughed. "He was a championship-level surfer a while back. He still goes out, mainly to help people wanting to learn."

"Think I'd like to learn. At home, guess that's our old home now, we've got this big, umm…What is it, mom?"

"Cherokee Reservoir."

"Yeah, the Reservoir. It's got a lot of water, but I don't think you can surf it. Maybe he can teach me. Mom, what do you think?"

"I think we need to get settled in your aunt's house, get new clothes, then we can think about surfing lessons. Deal?"

"If you say so." He lowered his head, not showing enthusiasm over her answer. He then raised his head. "Did you know mom is a professor?"

And I thought Charles could change subjects on the head of a pin. "I didn't know that, Luke. What does she teach?"

"English and books, umm…."

"Literature," Rose added. "Actually, I was only an associate professor at Walters State Community College in Morristown."

"How did you get there?" I asked.

"Got my master's in English from East Tennessee State University. After graduate school, I was fortunate to be offered the teaching job."

"That's where she met dad. He's a banker. They got married, had me, then didn't live happily ever after."

"Luke, I'm sure Chris doesn't want to hear all that."

The same couldn't have been said if Charles had been with us.

We'd made it to the front of Cindy's house. It was larger than the typical Folly house, was modern by island standards.

Rose patted my shoulder. "Thanks for walking us over. We could've found it on our own, but my big sis still looks after me like I'm a little kid. Suppose she always will." She glanced at Luke who was paying more attention to a couple of women walking down the street than to us. "Cindy wanted us to move in with her. I didn't want her hovering over us, big sister like, so that's why we rented. We don't have a choice now."

"Rose, I didn't mind walking with you. Sorry about the rude welcome you received. Not every newcomer's house burns."

"Thank you anyway. Could I get your number in case I think of anything else about the others in my building?"

We exchanged numbers. She thanked me again for walking her to Cindy's.

"Mom," Luke said, "can we get a dog like Mr. Dude's?"

"Maybe someday."

I left on that vague promise.

Chapter Five

After depositing Rose and Luke at Cindy's, I called the Chief to let her know her relatives were safely at her house.

"How are they?"

"A little shook, as you can imagine, but overall I think they're fine. We ran into Dude along the way. Pluto distracted Luke, which was good."

Cindy laughed. "I'd also wager Dude distracted my sister, the English professor."

"She said she taught literature, so I imagine she's familiar with the strange versions of the English language throughout history."

"She didn't study anything resembling Dudespeak."

"True. Anyway, they're safe at your place. Know what started the fire?"

"Nothing official until the experts say. I'd put money on arson."

"Why?"

"It went up too fast. The fire spread faster than normal unless it was accelerant fed."

"Any idea who may've set it?"

"Chris, give me a break. I'm standing here looking at what used to be a building. If the arsonist left a written confession, it's part of the smoldering crap."

"Do you know who besides your sister lived there?"

She gave an audible sigh. "Tell me again why I answered the damn phone."

"Cindy, you never told me the first time. I assumed it was to enjoy a conversation with one of your favorite residents."

"Yeah, but then it was you."

"Other residents?"

"Five of the units were rented. Fortunately, we haven't found any bodies. Unfortunately, none of the residents, other than Rose have come to claim their ashes. They're either still milling around the events on Center Street, are on the beach, or off-island. I don't know who they are. We're running plates on the cars in the lot. With luck, that'll give us some names."

"Rose told me she'd only met one resident. The guy in the second-floor center unit is named Ty. She didn't know his last name. The only Ty I know is Ty Striker, a young man who works at Bert's."

"Thank you, detective Chris."

"Just sharing what your sister said. What about the land-lord? Rose told me his name is Russell O'Leary. She doesn't think he lives on Folly."

"One of my guys tried to rent an apartment there a year ago. The units were full at the time, but he still had

O'Leary's number. I tried it, but with my luck, it's disconnected."

"You can call your house to get the number Rose has. It'd be more recent."

"Thank you again, detective Chris."

I wasn't anxious to go home, so I passed my cottage on my way to Bert's, Folly's iconic grocery that prides itself on never closing. Hurricanes are the only thing that've messed with that tradition. I cook about as often as I skydive, which is never, so having a grocery next door was one of the appealing features when I bought my retirement home. Besides never closing, Bert's carries everything from bungee cords to beer, neither of which I have a need, but between the two, I could find snacks, breakfast items high on calories, an occasional sandwich, plus numerous items to meet my unhealthy penchant for sweets.

Today, I wasn't looking for food. Ty Striker was my focus. He was behind the register waiting on a lady tugging a sad-looking beagle behind her. Ty met the description of the man Rose said lived in her building. He was about six-foot-two-inches tall, thin, in his early twenties, with a narrow face with a long nose. He looked like he could play Ichabod Crane in a prequel to "The Legend of Sleepy Hollow." His long black hair was pulled in a ponytail with a multi-colored scrunchie. A few wayward hairs sprang out the side.

He gave his customer change while wishing her a pleasant day, then noticed me standing off to the side.

"Mr. Landrum, want a dog treat?" he said with a wide smile exposing crooked front teeth.

Bert's kept a supply of treats, normally reserved for canines. For some reason, Ty offers me one most every time he sees me in the store. For the record, I've never accepted one.

"Ty, thanks for the offer, but I'll decline."

"Your loss. What brings you in? Coffee, cinnamon roll, candy bar?"

He knew me well.

"Actually, came to see you."

"That's a first. What about?"

"The fire."

Ty turned to an employee stocking a shelf behind him. "Roger, could you take over a few minutes? I need to find something for Mr. Landrum."

He did and Ty motioned me to follow him to the back of the store near the restroom.

"Mr. Landrum, since you mentioned fire, then said you came to see me, I assume you know I live, lived, in the building that went up in smoke."

"I heard someone named Ty lived there. I hoped it wasn't you, but thought I'd ask. Guess my hoping didn't make it not true."

He nodded. "I've been working since eleven this morning. I wanted to see the Christmas parade, but that wasn't to be. A fire engine and two police cars zoomed past, so I went outside where I saw smoke." He looked toward the door to the office, before whispering, "I sneaked out for fifteen minutes; ran up the street to see what was going on." He shook his head. "My building was one big bonfire. Everything in it had to be burnt to a crisp." He stopped and stared at the floor.

"I'm so sorry. What'd you do then?"

"What else could I do? I hightailed it back here. Figured I'd need every penny I could make. Mr. Landrum, I ain't got clothes other than what you see. Didn't have much furniture, but what I had is gone, gone."

"I hate to hear it."

"Got lucky though."

"How?"

"Lost."

"Lost what?"

"Lost, that's my cat. He's safe."

That led to more questions than I could ask in the limited time Ty had before he needed to get back to work.

"Ty, was Lost outside when the fire started?"

"No, was in my car. On cool days like today, I bring him to work. I leave him in the car. When I get breaks, I go out to talk to him. He doesn't get mad at me, or yell because I'm not checking someone out fast enough."

"I'm glad, umm, Lost is safe. Any idea what started the fire?"

"Not really. I was afraid to ask, but I think the building was probably a fire trap. It was old, sort of run down. The wiring wasn't too good."

"Where are you going to live now that your apartment's gone?"

"For a while, I can live in my car. I've done it before. It's not much, a twenty-year-old Miata. Heck, it's only two years younger than me. It's mighty squinchy to sleep in, but I've managed." He looked toward the front of the store. "I'd better get to work. Can't afford to lose this job since I don't have anywhere to stay that ain't on wheels."

I repeated I was sorry about his apartment.

"Don't worry, me and Lost will be okay."

Chapter Six

The phone jarred me awake. The clock revealed it was seven-fifteen but felt earlier since I had a hard time getting to sleep, having managed to drift off around three. Thoughts about the fire and how lucky the residents had been by not being home dominated those awake hours. Charles's name popped up on the screen.

"Good morning, Charles. Isn't it a little early to—"

"Why aren't you here?" he interrupted.

I wiped the sleep out of my eyes. "Where is here? Why would I be there, wherever it is?"

"The Dog. Duh."

"Now I know where, how about why?"

"Figured you'd want to know what I learned after you sashayed off with Cindy's sis and her youngin'."

After more than a decade of conversations with Charles, talks bordering on Dudespeak, the safest, possibly only response was to say, "I'm on my way."

"Thought so," Charles said before hanging up.

The Lost Dog Cafe was Folly's go-to location for three things: great breakfasts, excellent lunches, and rumors. As I've mentioned, my culinary skills coexist with nonexistent. If I want a meal that's not wrapped in aluminum foil or plastic wrap from Bert's, the Dog is my prime destination. I could almost walk to the colorful restaurant in my sleep. Today, I may be doing that since I was wiping sleep from my eyes as I headed to meet Charles. Fortunately, mild weather was hanging around. Sunday mornings were busy times for the restaurant located less than a block off Center Street. Two couples waited at the door for a table. Another couple leaned on the low railing decorated with a string of Christmas lights. I was glad Charles had commandeered a table. While it was unseasonably mild, it was too cool for dining on the two patios.

"About time you got here," said Amber Lewis, one of the restaurant's longest-term employees. She was one of the first people I met when I arrived on Folly. "Charles has been pestering me so much about when you would arrive, I thought I was going to have to go to your house to drag you out of bed."

The fifty-year-old server and I dated during my early years on Folly, then morphed into a close friendship. Along with her smile and talent for making customers feel at ease, Amber was one of the island's top sharers of rumors.

"Amber, I didn't know I was coming until Charles disturbed my sleep a half-hour ago."

"I know. He said he couldn't fathom why you weren't here when he showed up the second we opened."

Charles was at a table near the back of the restaurant

watching my interaction with Amber. He glanced at his wrist where normal people wore a watch. Charles, anything but normal, didn't own one. The wrist glance was his way of saying I was late. He was wearing a navy-blue long-sleeve T-shirt with Wheaton in orange on the front.

"What took you so long?"

"Good morning, Charles. Nice day, isn't it?"

Amber delivered a steaming-hot mug of coffee before Charles could continue chiding me for being late, which, of course, I wasn't. She asked if I wanted yogurt for breakfast, her effort to get me to eat healthier. I said French toast, my effort to resist her healthy suggestion. She smiled, feigned shock at the selection I chose for breakfast ninety percent or more of the time, then left to place my order.

Charles said, "Want to know about my shirt?"

My friend had a larger selection of T-shirts than all the T-shirt stores on Folly combined. I stopped asking about them years ago. That didn't stop him from sharing more than I wanted to know.

"No."

"Wheaton College, it's in Illinois. Know what it's got?"

Don't say you weren't warned.

"No."

"One of the oldest and largest Christmas festivals in the good old US of A."

"Is that why you wanted me to meet you?"

"Nope. That was a bonus, something to brighten your holiday spirit."

Charles took a bite of bacon, one of the few bites left on his plate, reinforcing he'd been here a while, then said, "Ready for the reason I called this meeting?"

I didn't even know it was a meeting. "Absolutely."

"While you were strolling through the streets of Folly with the police chief's lovely sister and her son, I was plying my well-honed detective skills at the site of the former, six-unit apartment building."

"I'm certain the Chief was thrilled with your help."

"Sarcasm doesn't suit you this early in the day."

Neither does trivia about Wheaton College, I thought.

I shrugged. "What'd you learn?"

"That's more like it. The main thing I learned was who lived there." He took another bite, then nodded like he'd discovered Colonel Sanders's fried chicken secret ingredients.

"Plan on sharing who?"

"Sure, once I finish enjoying knowing something you don't know."

Amber arrived with my breakfast allowing Charles to enjoy his knowledge a moment longer.

I poured syrup on my French toast while Charles finished gloating and started naming the residents.

"First, Janice Raque, the lady you accused of killing the bookie."

Charles and I met Janice months earlier when she became a prime suspect in the murder of a bookie whose body Charles and I unfortunately discovered. We also managed to catch the killer letting Janice off the hook. At the time, she was married, then her husband left her for a younger woman. After the divorce, she was forced to move out of her condo, but I didn't know where she'd landed.

"How'd you learn she lived there?"

"Outstanding detective work."

I stared at him.

"Okay, I was standing behind the police line when Janice tapped me on the arm, pointed to where the second floor used to be, and said, 'Oh my God, that was my apartment."

I grinned. "Wow, that's outstanding detective work."

"Sarcasm still doesn't suit you."

I smiled. "Who else?"

"Someone else you know. Would you believe Neil Wilson?"

I'd met Neil about the same time I'd become acquainted with Janice. In fact, he was another suspect in the bookie's murder. Neil's in his late forties, a former college football player, and built like someone I wouldn't want to argue with. He split his work career between being a bouncer in a bar in downtown Charleston, and part-time cook on Folly at Cal's Country Bar and Burgers.

"Neil and Janice in the same building. Weird."

"Neil lived there long before the bookie was killed, Janice moved in because it was the only place she could afford."

"I suppose you used your outstanding detective talents to learn he lived there."

"You're catching on. In fact, I used the age-old detective technique of developing an informant."

"Which means?"

"Listen closely, you can learn something from this. Ready?"

I nodded.

"I said, 'Janice, who else lived in the building?'"

I laughed, skipped the sarcasm, and jumped right to, "Who else?"

"That's where my skills deserted me."

I shared what I'd learned from Ty. I didn't attribute my knowledge to any detective skills.

Charles said, "Then, there was one other apartment, the one on the far side of the second floor. No one I talked to knew who rented it. Janice didn't know her name, but said it was a young, black woman. Janice is nearly sixty, so to her, young could be anyone between twenty and fifty. Janice didn't know much about the mystery woman. She saw her leaving the apartment a few times. Drives a black Dodge Ram pickup truck."

"Good job, Charles."

"You being sarcastic again?"

"Not this time. That's a lot more than Cindy knew when I called to tell her Rose and Luke were at her house."

"What'd she tell you?"

"Not much. She speculated the fire started in the vacant apartment in the middle of the first floor. She was fairly certain it was arson."

"A guy with the Charleston Fire Marshall Division was pulling in as I was leaving."

"Cindy called them."

"Speaking of Cindy, tell me about her sister."

I shared some of what I'd learned about Rose during the walk to Cindy's house. Charles, being Charles, asked me approximately seven thousand questions ranging from what Rose taught, not just what classes but how many students were in each class, why she got a divorce, what her ex-husband did for a living, ending with did she and Luke have pets when they were in Tennessee.

I was never happier to see anyone more than when Amber returned to refill our mugs. She poured coffee, then said, "Guys, where're the residents of the building going to live? Christmas is around the corner. Imagine how horrible it is for them."

I knew the answer for one of the tenants, but only one.

Chapter Seven

I left Charles at the Dog where he stopped to talk with a couple waiting for a table. They had a young border collie making it impossible for Charles to pass without talking to the canine, interrogating the couple about the enthusiastic pup's name, where the couple was from, and I don't know what else, since I told him I'd see him later then left him with the couple who I suspected were there for breakfast rather than an inquisition.

It was still warm for December, so I walked to the apartment building, more accurately, to what was left of the building. The smell of burnt debris assailed my nose a block before I got to the site. Part of the rear of the building and the right side were the only remnants of the structure standing. The roof, front wall, plus most of the left side of the building had collapsed and were barely recognizable in the rubble. Puddles of water from the firefighters' efforts had settled in low-lying sections of the ruins. Few items were identifiable. When the second floor burned through, refrigerators and stoves landed close to the ones in the first-floor units. Burned wood or steel frames were all that was left of the furniture. Glassware was shattered from the heat or from falling from the second floor. One item caught my attention. Inside what had been Rose and Luke's apartment, there was a blackened Christmas tree stand. The tree I pictured decked out with lights and ornaments, had been cremated.

It was hard to comprehend how five households were turned to worthless remnants in minutes. It may've been my imagination, but I thought I smelled gasoline, possibly the accelerant used to spread the fire making it impossible to save much. It was a sad sight to see anytime, but this close to Christmas, it was heartbreaking.

I was so focused on the devastation I didn't notice a black Dodge Ram pickup parked in the far corner of the deserted lot. The windows were tinted, but from the angle of the sun, I saw the outline of someone in the driver's seat. I remembered what Janice Raque told Charles about the building's still-unnamed resident, and what Cindy had said about a Dodge Ram being in the lot during the fire.

As I moved away from the rubble, the truck's door opened. An African-American female stepped out and smiled. She was in her late twenties or early thirties, thin, roughly five-foot-three, with a short afro, and wearing a dark-gray sweatshirt and black jeans. She hesitated before taking a couple of steps in my direction.

"Hi, I'm Chris Landrum." I pointed at the pile of burnt wood. "You lived there?"

Her smile turned to a look of surprise. "How'd you know?"

"I wasn't certain, but someone told me one of the residents drove a truck like yours."

"Oh." She stepped closer and held out her hand. "I'm Noelle Ward. Lived on the second floor."

"I'm terribly sorry about your apartment."

She shook her head. "Not nearly as sorry as I am. Do you live around here?"

"Near Bert's. Live here long?"

"Year next month."

"Did you lose everything?"

She nodded. "What you see is what I have left."

"Again, I'm sorry."

She turned to stare at what was left of the building, slowly shook her head, then barely above a whisper said, "Can't say I wasn't warned."

I wasn't sure I heard her correctly. "Sorry, what?"

"It's not important. Did you hear if everyone is safe?"

Not important wasn't my impression, but I didn't push.

"Yes, no one was in the building when it started. Where were you during the fire?"

"Researching something I'm writing. I was walking along the beach, almost made it to the west end of the island. I didn't know about the fire until late yesterday when I got back. Quite a shock, but glad no one was hurt."

"What are you writing?"

She smiled. "A novel."

No one's ever said that to me. "Your first?"

"Yes."

"What's it about?"

"Really want to know?"

"Sure."

"It's a murder mystery, set on a small imaginary island in Georgia. I picture it a place like Folly. That's why I moved here. I wanted to get my toes wet living and hanging around somewhere like where my novel takes place. You a reader?"

I smiled. "Afraid not. The newspaper is the extent of my reading material. I do have a friend who claims to have read every mystery novel written since Gutenberg."

She laughed. "A man after my own heart."

The more Noelle talked about her book, the more she relaxed, the more her voice, soft-spoken until now, became filled with confidence.

"If you've been around here a year, I'm surprised you haven't met him. His name's Charles Fowler."

She leaned on her truck's fender. "Don't recall the name, but I may have seen him. I'm terrible with names. He works on Folly?"

"He's retired. Occasionally, he helps some of the restaurants clean in the busy season. He also delivers local packages for the surf shop. Delivers them on his bike."

"Sounds like Mr. Fowler could be a character in my book."

"There's no doubt he's a character. If you're still around and he's with me, I'll introduce him. What are your plans now?"

"No idea. I spent last night in my truck."

"Sorry."

She smiled. "Don't be, the space in that big ole' Dodge is larger than the apartment I lived in while attending college. I still want to live over here. It's helping with my plot. You don't know of any little apartments for rent, do you? Don't want it to be too nice. My protagonist lives in a place I describe as a dump. That's the kind of apartment I'm looking for."

"Off the top of my head, I don't. If you don't mind

giving me your number, I'll let you know if I hear of something."

"I'd appreciate it."

"Will you be okay until you find a new place?"

"Yes. Got a decent day job so I can buy clothes, food, other stuff. I'll be fine."

"Where do you work?"

I realized I was sounding like Charles with all the questions.

"Ad agency in downtown Charleston."

"Then I suppose writing comes easy."

She chuckled. "Yes and no. I have a degree in English, so I know how to string words together. Trouble is I'm good at writing copy for an ad or a television commercial where the word count can often be counted on my fingers plus toes. For my novel, I'll have to fill three hundred pages with words."

I couldn't imagine even writing enough to fill the television commercial.

"Sounds like a challenge, Noelle."

"You're telling me." She laughed. "Actually, my real name's Imani Marshall. Noelle's my pen name. With my background in advertising, I assure you, fewer people would buy a book written by Imani than Noelle."

Something was bothering me, so I figured that since she was more relaxed than when she got out of the truck, I could ask. "That makes sense. Got one more question. A little while ago when we were talking about when you learned of the fire, you said something like can't say I wasn't warned. What'd you mean?"

Her pleasant expression disappeared. "It's nothing important."

I didn't believe it but didn't know her enough to push for an explanation. "Okay. I'd better let you get on your way. I've enjoyed talking to you. Again, I'm sorry about your apartment."

Her smile returned, but not with the wattage from earlier.

"You too, Mr. Landrum."

She gave me her number. I promised to let her know if I heard about an apartment for rent.

She returned to her truck, slowly pulled out of the lot, then turned toward town. I watched her go, with one large unanswered question nagging me. What did she mean when she said she'd been warned?

Chapter Eight

After talking with two people who lost near everything and were spending nights in their vehicle, I began wondering about the others. Rose and Luke had somewhere to go, but what about Neil and Janice? I called Chief LaMond on the walk home.

"This better be good. This is my day off. Lo and behold, the wonderful, thoughtful, love of my life, brilliant hubby took me to brunch at Poogan's Porch. He—"

I interrupted, "He's listening, right?"

"Duh," Cindy said, answering my question. "He said it'd be a good way for me to get out of Dodge, or Folly, so I could enjoy a peaceful Sunday meal without being distracted by some idiot determined to ruin my day. Did I mention this is my day off—like in day to not work?"

"Sweetie," I heard Larry say in the background, "you may want to let him tell you why he called."

Cindy sighed. "Okay, Mr. Pest, what did I do to deserve a call on my day off?"

I didn't want to tell her after listening to her rant, I'd almost forgotten why I called.

"Chief, a couple of things. First, I was at the site of the fire where I ran into the lady who owned the Dodge pickup that was in the lot during the fire. Did you get a chance to talk to her?"

"Mr. Nosy Citizen, I also have a couple of things. First, why in hell were you at the site of the fire? In addition to nosing in police business and bumbling around catching killers, are you adding catching arsonists to your resume?"

"Chief, of course not. I can't add that to my resume until I catch one."

Cindy made a noise reminding me of a braying horse, then said, "Larry, order me another beer. I'm going to need it. Okay, Chris, the second thing is no, I haven't talked to the owner of the Dodge. What did you learn from her?"

Regardless of how hard a time Cindy gives me, she listens to what I say. I shared my conversation with Imani enlightening Cindy about Imani's pen name. I also gave her Noelle's number in case she wanted to contact her. I didn't share Noelle's comment about being warned since I didn't know what she'd meant. Cindy asked me to repeat Imani's pen name, saying her secretary, aka Larry, was better at running a hardware store than taking notes. I repeated it then added what Noelle said about writing a murder mystery.

"Chris, if you pester me again on my day off, Noelle will have a real murder to write about."

I took the subtle hint, apologized for calling, then said I hoped she enjoyed the rest of her brunch.

"Whoa, Mr. Senior Citizen, you said there were a couple

of reasons you called on, in case I haven't mentioned it, my day off. What's number two?"

Told you she listened.

"I know where Rose and Luke are staying, but I was worried about the others. Any idea what's happening to them?"

"I told all of them they could stay at your house. I warned them not to expect a bed and breakfast. A bed, maybe. Breakfast, not a chance."

"Funny. Seriously, know anything about their plans?"

"I called the Red Cross yesterday; talked with a nice man in their disaster relief and recovery program. They'll provide money for food and will put the displaced residents up for two nights in one of three Charleston hotels. I've already told Neil Wilson, Janice Raque, and Ty Striker. Rose and Luke won't need help. Now that some busybody gave me the name of the other person on my day off, I'll contact her."

"Good. While I'm thinking about it, did you ever get in touch with the building's owner?"

"That's three things," she said before hanging up.

Must be her day off.

———

The next morning, I called Burl Costello, a friend who's pastor of First Light Church, Folly's newest house of worship; or more accurately, place of worship, since most of First Light's services are held on the beach. My call wasn't related to the church, but to Hope House, a halfway house Preacher Burl started two years ago. The large house was donated by a wealthy member of First Light under the condition Burl rents its rooms to people whom he felt needed the assist to get back to being productive members of the community. I asked Burl if he could spare a few minutes. He said he could but only if I shared a cup of coffee with him. He drove a hard bargain, but I relented.

Thirty minutes later, I was standing on the porch of the large, fifty-plus-year-old, wood-frame house on East Erie Avenue. White Christmas lights were strung around the door frame, giving it a holiday feel although the house had seen better days.

"Welcome, Brother Chris," Burl said as he waved me in. "Coffee's brewing."

Burl was in his mid-fifties, no more than five-foot-five, shaped like a football sitting on a kicking tee, topped by a face covered with a milk-chocolate colored mustache and balding head.

I followed him through the long center hallway to the large country-style kitchen.

"It's good to see you again," Burl said, as he poured my coffee and refilled his mug. "I've missed you at church."

At best, I was an irregular attendee at First Light.

"Sorry," I said with little enthusiasm.

"No need to apologize to me, Brother Chris. I'm not the one keeping score."

Time to move along.

"Burl, I'm sure you heard about the apartment building fire on East Ashley."

"It would've been hard to live on Folly without hearing of the conflagration. We had a prayer yesterday and a special offering to give to the survivors most in need. Brother Bernard is taking the love offering to the fire department this morning so they can distribute it to those displaced."

Bernard Prine was one of the Hope House residents I'd known for a couple of years. He's a military veteran suffering from PTSD, more recently called PTSI, post-traumatic stress injury, to lessen the stigma associated with the word disorder. Regardless of its name, Bernard had been kicked out of several homeless shelters for fighting before Burl worked his magic, making him feel like an important part of Hope House.

"Speaking of people in need, Preacher, do you have vacancies? I know two of the residents who're sleeping in their vehicles. There are two others I don't know about."

He took a sip, shook his head, and said, "Brother Chris, I'm saddened to say all six of my rooms are occupied. Two rooms that had been vacant were filled last week. Unless something unexpected occurs, I don't know any residents who've found other accommodations."

"Sorry to hear that, Preacher."

"Sorry to have to convey that news. But, Brother Chris, you know I'm an optimist. I have faith God, possibly working in strange and mysterious ways, will look over them to provide suitable accommodations."

"Preacher, I wish I had that much faith."

Burl smiled. "Ah, Brother Chris, we talk about things like faith on Sunday mornings. Perhaps a refresher would be helpful."

I mimicked his smile. "Subtle, Preacher Burl."

His smile turned to a laugh. "That's why I get paid the big bucks, Brother Chris." He turned serious. "I will keep the displaced residents in my prayers, but if that isn't enough by itself, I will enquire with others to see if there are alternatives we currently are unaware of."

"Thank you, Preacher. And, thanks for the coffee."

"Brother Chris, my coffee pot is always available to you."

Before I reached the car, the phone rang. Cindy's name appeared on the screen.

"Good morning, Chief."

"Did I tell you yesterday was my day off? Larry took me to Poogan's Porch where I had Chicken and Waffles."

I chuckled. "I believe you mentioned it."

"It was fantastic except for an exasperating call from one of Folly's nosiest residents. Can you believe he interrupted my scrumptious brunch to ask if I'd gotten ahold of the owner of the building that disappeared the other day?"

"A Chief's work is never done."

"You can say that again. In case you're interested, the answer is not yet."

"Where is he?"

"Could be swimming in the Mediterranean Sea, skydiving over the Grand Canyon, hell, for all I know he could be floating around in the International Space Station. What I know is he's not answering the number he'd given Rose."

"So, what now?"

"I'll tell you the other bit of trivia I called for, then hang up so I can go to a budget meeting with the Mayor, a dream come true."

"The bit of trivia is?"

"The fire was arson. Don't ask, I don't know who set it."

Chapter Nine

One of Charles's numerous quirks was if I learned something he didn't know and didn't tell him in, oh, let's say, three flaps of a hummingbird's wing, a bucket of grief would follow. I'd exceeded that timeframe since meeting Noelle, so a call was overdue.

He was wheezing as he answered the phone.

"Where are you?" I asked.

"Jogging around the island."

I could count on fewer than one finger the number of times Charles had been jogging.

"Jogging?"

"Okay, maybe a brisk walk. Why?"

He took a brisk walk slightly more often than he jogged, but I let it go. "Where are you?"

"Getting ready to plop my rear on the picnic table at the Folly River Park."

Folly River Park is a small park bordered by the Folly River, Center Street, and East Indian Avenue. It's the site of art fairs throughout the year, but shines, figuratively and literally, during the holiday season as the location of Folly's official Christmas tree surrounded by large, colorfully lit seasonal displays.

"Plop down. I'll join you in about fifteen minutes."

Ten minutes later, I spotted him on the picnic table. He would've been hard to overlook wearing a cardinal red, long-sleeve sweatshirt with Arkansas Razorbacks and a fierce-looking hog on the front. He also wore a Tilley hat with nothing written on it, jeans, and tennis shoes that looked like they could've jogged hundreds of miles, although not on Charles's feet.

I nudged him to move over then scooted beside him on the table.

He stared at the Christmas tree, then said, "Why do bad things always happen at Christmas?"

"Bad things happen all the time. They seem worse this time of year."

"That sucks."

"Yes, but look at all the good things happening, especially during the Christmas season."

He glanced at the tree, then turned to me. "I thought I was the half-full kind of guy. You going to tell those folks who lived in the apartment building good things are happening?"

My friend had always been that half-full guy. In the last couple of years, he'd experienced some personal losses that jaded his outlook.

"Charles, I agree. Losing most everything was terrible. On the other hand, no one was injured. Cindy confirmed the fire was set which made it spread faster than would've been normal. They were lucky not to be home."

"When did the Chief tell you that?"

"Right before I called you."

I hoped that would get me off the hook, that is until I tell him about meeting the writer yesterday.

"If it was arson, why?"

I resisted the temptation to tell him to burn the building. Instead, I said, "What do you mean?"

"Whoever set it did it during the day when the odds were great its residents wouldn't be home or would've been awake enough to get out once they knew the building was ablaze. If the arsonist wanted to hurt or kill someone, wouldn't he or she have set it in the middle of the night when the intended victim was asleep?" He glanced at the tree again before turning back to me. "So, why set the fire?"

That reminded me of what Noelle shared about being warned.

"What if the arsonist wanted to scare one of the residents, not hurt him or her?"

"It would've scared the heebie-jeebies out of me if I'd seen everything I owned go up in smoke."

"Cindy also said she couldn't find the building's owner. What—"

"Whoa," he interrupted, "when did she say that?"

Don't say I didn't warn you about his quirk.

"Same time she confirmed it was arson. May I finish?"

He harrumphed then motioned me to continue.

I said, "What if the landlord torched his building?"

"Insurance?"

"Yes. It would've been a good time to do it when fewer tenants were at risk."

"How are we going to find out?"

"Charles, the police are looking at all possibilities. They'll figure it out."

"They can't even find the landlord. How do you think they'll prove he started the fire?"

"They'll find him. I didn't say it was the landlord, but it's my best guess."

"What about one of the tenants starting it?"

"Why?"

"Get out of paying rent. One of them may've been behind, figuring he or she wouldn't have to pay if the apartment wasn't there."

"That's a possibility," I said but thought it unlikely since they'd be homeless as a result.

A man walking a boxer passed us on the paved path through the park. Charles, who could never let a dog pass without a brief conversation, hopped off the table then knelt to say a few words to the canine. He apparently ran out of canine-Charles conversation. The man and his dog continued around the park; Charles returned to the table.

"Where were the tenants when the fire started?" he asked as he watched the dog walk away.

"Ty was at Bert's. Rose and her son were watching the parade." I took a deep breath, preparing for an explosion, and said, "Noelle was walking on the beach. We don't—"

Charles's hand flew in front of my face. "Stop! Noelle?"

"I was walking by the site of the fire yesterday afternoon and saw the pickup truck that was there during the fire. The driver was looking at the ruins. Her name is Noelle Ward, actually, her name is Imani Marshall, but she goes by Noelle."

I paused anticipating Charles interrupting.

"Well, go on," he said, hinting he's not always predictable.

I gave him a brief bio on Noelle, including why she was using a pen name. Charles interrupted me twice to make sure she didn't already have published novels. Said if she did, he would've read them. I exhausted everything I knew about Noelle, repeated it twice before Charles felt he had enough information.

"Okay," he said, "what about Neil. Where was he?"

I told him I didn't know, then gave him the same answer when he asked if I knew where Janice was during the fire.

"Wonder how we're going to find out where they were?"

"Suppose we could use one of your well-honed detective skills. We could ask them."

Charles grabbed his phone and punched in a number.

"Yo, Cal, this is Charles, yeah, Charles Fowler. What other Charles do you know? Right. Is Neil there?"

Apparently, he was talking to our friend, Cal Ballew, at his bar where Neil was a part-time cook. Charles tapped his finger on the table while Cal said something. I could tell from the intensity of his tapping it wasn't to Charles's liking.

"Okay, thanks anyway."

He returned the phone to his pocket and shook his head. "Off today. Comes in at three tomorrow. You have Neil's number?"

"Why didn't you ask that before calling Cal's?"

"Well, do you?"

I scrolled through my contacts, tapped on Neil's number, then handed the phone to Charles. He didn't have as much luck as he had with Cal. He handed the phone back to me saying there was no answer.

Charles smiled and asked if I had Janice's number. I told

him no before he proclaimed the day a total failure. His half-empty mood was back.

It went more downhill after he asked where the tenants would live.

"Rose and Luke will be fine," I said. "Cindy said the Red Cross was putting the others up for a couple of nights in a Charleston hotel."

"They think the landlord will wiggle his nose and a new building will rise from the ashes before two nights in a motel are used up?"

"That's all they can do."

"What about the others?" He snapped his fingers. "Got it. They could move to Hope House?"

I readied myself for another burst of irritation, then told him about my conversation with Burl.

"Crap. Christmas is around the corner and I doubt any of them could fit in a manger, even if we could find one for rent."

I interpreted that comment to be more out of frustration than my failure to tell him about meeting Burl. He got a far-away look in his eyes, a look I'd learned over the years not to interrupt.

He snapped his fingers a second time. "Got an idea."

I waited for him to share. When he didn't, I said, "What?"

"My apartment's too small for me to live in much less adding someone else."

Charles was right. In addition to being small, he'd added bookshelves to almost every wall, filled them with enough reading material to fill a small-town library. Other than his bed, every horizontal surface was covered with books, including much of the floor.

"I agree."

He smiled. "Your house is another story. Think about that extra bedroom that's only holding a computer with a printer. Acres of empty space. There'd be plenty of room for one of the poor, sad, displaced tenants to hang his hat until better accommodations come available." He nodded. "Great idea, if I say so myself."

I'd come to the same conclusion last night but didn't know if I was ready for a housemate. I'd lived alone for thirty years. Every time I'd considered other options, like adding a spouse, I broke out in cold sweats.

"Charles, there's no bed, besides, who's to say one of them would be interested?"

"You're right. Heck, I'm sure Ty is thrilled to be living like a pretzel in his Miata. Noelle must be feeling like a queen living in her pickup. We don't know anything about Neil or Janice. Think about it. I'll see if I can twist arms to help the others out. Surely I can guilt somebody by playing the Christmas card."

"I'll think about it."

"Good, you can tell me your decision tomorrow when we go to Cal's for a burger, a drink, a powwow with Neil."

Chapter Ten

The next morning began with me heading next door to grab a cinnamon Danish and cup of complimentary coffee. It was at least ten degrees colder than the last two days, so I pulled the collar of my lightweight jacket up around my neck. Over the years, I'd been tempted to buy a heavier coat, but refused telling myself Folly Beach was in the South so I wouldn't need anything warmer. Several times over the years, I'd regretted my stubbornness. This was one of those times.

Ty's Miata was parked in the lot between my house and Bert's. I was tempted to peek in to see if his cat was there. Instead, I rushed to the warmth of the store. Ty was behind the counter where three people waited to check out. He smiled when he saw me then went back to giving a woman change. My feet automatically took me to the case where oversized gooey delights would tempt me. I put a Danish in a paper bag then proceeded to the large coffee urn and filled a cup. By the time I made it to the register, Ty's customers were gone.

"Morning, Ty," I said as I put money on the counter for the Danish.

Ty's smile widened. "Mr. Landrum, it's a wonderful day."

His attitude was better than mine would be under similar circumstances.

"You seem happy this morning. Win the lottery?"

He continued to smile. "Afraid not, Mr. Landrum. I'm thankful Lost and I wasn't hurt in the fire. Things can always be worse, be worse."

"Is Lost in your car?"

"Not today, it's too cold for the little fellow. Left him in the hotel where the good folks from Red Cross are letting me bunk."

I knew the answer, but asked anyway, "How long will you be there?"

"Tonight will be it. It was nice of them to give me two nights."

"What'll happen then?"

"Suppose I'll move back in my car. Not quite luxury digs, but beggars can't be choosers, be choosers. I think that's how the saying goes."

A woman carrying a loaf of bread appeared behind me. I stepped aside so she could pay. Ty took her money, told her to have a wonderful day, then turned to me.

"Mr. Landrum, would you let me know if you hear of any cheap apartments for rent. Lost needs a better place to live than the car."

"What about you?"

He smiled. "Wouldn't mind it myself."

"I'll keep an eye out."

"Lost would appreciate it."

At the risk of sounding like Charles, curiosity got me to ask, "How'd you come up with the name Lost?"

He smiled. "Not the first time I've heard that question. Want the long or short version?"

I looked around and didn't see anyone vying for Ty's attention. "Whichever you have time for."

"I don't suppose you know anything about me other than what you see in here."

"True."

"I moved from Baltimore a little over a year ago. I came to Folly with a couple of friends I worked with at a roofing company. Tell you something, Mr. Landrum, slapping roofs on buildings when it's ninety degrees isn't high on the list of fun jobs, but see, I sort of barely got through high school. They said I was smart enough to go to college, but since I had a better time not being in school than when I was there, I figured I wouldn't be good for college. College wouldn't be good for me. That may not have been one of my better decisions. Anyway, my buds and me were coming here to vacation, surf, drink beer, then, drink more beer. Two days before we were to go back to roofing, we came in here to buy beer." He hesitated, then smiled. "I was standing right where you are when I saw a girl working behind the deli counter. Heard her tell someone her name was Aimee." His smile widened. "Mr. Landrum, she was the cutest girl I'd ever seen. I mean ever."

By now, I assumed, hoped, this was the long version of how Lost got his name. I took a sip of coffee and was tempted to pull some of the Danish out of the bag. I didn't but waited for Ty to continue.

"The next morning, I left my roommates sleeping. I came here, asked if the manager was around. The clerk pointed me his direction, so I asked if he was hiring. Figured it would be the best way to get to know Aimee, Aimee Mason I learned. Suppose you figured out he was hiring."

I nodded.

"Aimee and me got to talking when we were on overlapping shifts, and—"

"Ty!" someone yelled from the back of the store. "Let Caroline take the register. I need your help unloading boxes."

Ty sighed. "The rest of the story will have to wait. Sorry, Mr. Landrum."

"Ty, before you go, do you have a number for your landlord?"

He pulled out his wallet, took out a folded piece of paper, and handed it to me. I unfolded the paper where I found the name Russell O'Leary plus a phone number. I put the number in my phone, returned the paper to Ty, then said we'd talk later.

Sitting at my seldom-used kitchen table, I ate the Danish while thinking about how unaffected Ty was about what was in my mind a horrible situation. I admired his outlook. I also wondered if the number he'd given me was the one the Chief had been using to reach the landlord. Today wasn't her day off, so I figured it'd be safe to call to give her the number.

"Good morning, one of my less-neurotic friends. You calling to apologize for interrupting one of my few days off?"

I smiled. "If it'll make you feel better, yes."

"Apology accepted. You going to say something now that'll need another apology?"

"Never, Chief. I was talking with Ty Striker a little while ago. He gave me a number for Russell O'Leary. I thought if it was different than the one you had; it may help you get in touch with the landlord."

She hesitated before speaking. "Just curious, why in holy hell were you asking Ty for the landlord's number? You want to rent an apartment or buy a bucket of soot?"

"Chief, you were having trouble reaching him. I wanted to help."

"Chris, don't treat me like you're talking to one of my dodo-brain officers. You're nosing in police business. Again."

Nothing would be gained by denying it. She wouldn't believe me. Neither would I. "Want the number?"

"Don't need it. I talked to O'Leary yesterday. Neil Wilson gave me a number I didn't have."

"What'd you learn from O'Leary?"

"Give me one reason I should answer that question?"

"Because—"

"Never mind. The only acceptable answer is because you'll pester me up to my eyeballs if I don't. I need that as much as I need the mayor threatening to fire me unless I start talking and acting like a police chief."

Mayor Newman had been on her case for as long as she'd been Chief. He knew she wasn't about to change, but that hadn't stopped him.

"What'd you learn from O'Leary?"

"Crap on a cucumber, Chris. Do you ever give up?"

See what the mayor meant?

I repeated, "O'Leary?"

"He swore he didn't know anything about the fire until the next day. Claims he was in Atlanta attending a seminar on buying real estate, getting filthy rich, without having to put any money down, or something like that."

"How'd he learn about the fire?"

"Claims he got back from Atlanta, drove by the building, where he perceptively noticed it was no longer there."

"Did you ask if he knew anyone who might've had reason to start the fire?"

"Gee, Chris, why didn't we professional investigators think to ask that."

Got it.

"What'd he say?"

"Claims he didn't know anyone."

"Cindy, why do I have the impression you don't believe his story?"

"What makes you say that?"

"You've used the word claims three times sharing his version."

"Damn, it's annoying you actually listen to me. Annoying and scary."

"Well?"

"I asked him the name of the seminar he allegedly attended. He couldn't remember. I asked when he got to Atlanta. He said a few days before the seminar. If I asked you that kind of question, wouldn't you name a specific day rather than 'a few days'? It's hard to judge someone's behavior over the phone, but my gut tells me he was lying about some of what he was saying."

"What next?"

"I'm going to call him later to schedule a face-to-face."

"Good luck."

"I'll need it if I want him to confess to torching his building."

Chapter Eleven

Cal Ballew took ownership of the bar eight years ago after Gregory Brile, the former owner, did what many people only dream of doing. He killed an attorney. Apparently, doing rather than dreaming has serious consequences. Gregory is in prison. The name of the bar switched from GB's to Cal's. The new owner, now in his mid-seventies, had spent most of his adult life traveling around the South, living out of his car, while playing his brand of traditional country music at any venue that would have him. He was performing at GB's when the owner moved from a comfortable house to a less-comfortable prison cell. Cal reluctantly took over even though he knew as much about owning a bar as a gecko knows about playing Chinese checkers.

Because of his decades on the road with nowhere to go on Christmas, when Cal took over, he was determined to hold an annual Christmas party so others who might share experiences similar to his would feel at home; a place where they could enjoy the spirit, fellowship, and calories of the holiday. His party has grown each year. It was now one of the highlights of the year, not only for those who had nowhere to go but for many of us who loved to share the joyous event with Cal. The singer who treated his patrons to a handful of sets during the week wasn't getting wealthy with the business but squirreled away money throughout the year so his Christmas party could provide free food and drinks to all comers.

I'd told Charles I'd meet him at Cal's but hadn't set a time. I was surprised he wasn't there when I arrived so he could tell me I was late. What was there brought a smile to my face. Four, seven-foot-tall artificial Christmas trees anchored the corners of the room. Multiple strands of colorful lights were attached to each non-moving vertical surface, more dangled from the ceiling. The bar spent most of the year looking tired, to put it kindly, but perked up come December. There were a dozen tables, plus a handful of barstools in front of the wooden bar on the side of the room. A twelve-by-twenty-foot laminate dance floor abutted a small stage in front of the room. The rest of the floor was covered with fraying indoor/outdoor carpet.

Seasonal sounds of Bing Crosby's "White Christmas" were coming from the antique Wurlitzer jukebox parked on a corner of the stage. Crosby's mellow voice competed with the country voice of Cal who was standing behind the bar drying a glass with a red, white, and blue bar towel. The owner was six-foot-three, toothpick thin with a spine that curved forward from bending down to a microphone plus living out of the back seat of his car for decades. Long, gray hair poked out from around the Stetson that'd traveled with him for more than forty years. In deference to the season, a strand of battery-operated, colorful lights was strung around the hat's crown. If Santa was anorexic, didn't have a beard, didn't wear a red suit, and didn't ride around the world transported by reindeer, Cal could be his double. I suspect Cal had a better singing voice, although I'd never heard Santa sing.

"Well if it isn't one of Santa's wise men," Cal said, mixing Christmas stories. He waved his hand around the room. "What do you think of this year's decorations?"

I thought they were overboard, but the same as last year. That wouldn't have been the correct answer, so I said, "Incredible, Cal, incredible."

"So you noticed the extra lights I've strung from the ceiling?"

Not really. I repeated, "Incredible."

Cal looked to see if anyone was nearby. No one was. "Truth be told, Neil did all the light stringing. This old broken-down body and ladders don't mix."

"Cal, it doesn't matter who decorated, it looks great. Would Neil happen to be here?"

He moved his head in the direction of the small kitchen. "In back, fixin' burgers for that table of guys by the wall, the ones looking like undertakers dressed in those suits. Must be a convention at the Tides."

Gene Autry began singing one of probably a thousand performers' versions of "Jingle Bells," as Cal handed me a glass of Cabernet, one I hadn't requested. He had my number.

"Chris, know what Charles told me about that song?"

Of course, I didn't, so I shook my head before taking a sip.

"Some cat wrote it back in eighteen-hundred-something as a Thanksgiving song. Can you believe that?"

If there was some archaic bit of trivia involved, I'd believe it. I limited my response to, "Who would've guessed?"

Neil walked out of the kitchen carrying a tray holding three hamburgers, two orders of fries, with an order of onion rings vying for space.

Neil said, "Hey, Chris."

Cal pointed to the table of men who ordered the burgers. Neil took the hint and headed their way.

Cal watched him move around two other tables. "You know about the fire at Neil's place, don't you?"

I nodded.

"Of course, you do, pard. You know everything bad that happens here."

I wouldn't have put it that way.

"How's Neil taking it?"

"Not as good as he wants everyone to think. He comes across as a big ole bruiser, living up to his part-time bouncer job downtown."

Neil could play that role well. He was six-three or four, in his late forties, looks like a former football player whose muscle turned to fat after his playing days ended. I remembered him coming across the way Cal described him earlier this year when he was a suspect in the bookie's murder. In fact, it was Cal who'd told me about a temper tantrum Neil had during a confrontation with the bookie.

I said, "That's the image he portrays."

"Dig deeper, pard, you'll find a big teddy bear. The boy's torn up about the fire, not just because it left him without a bed, but he feels horrible about the others who lost everything." Cal watched Neil as he left the food at the table and headed our way. "Don't tell him I said anything, okay, pard?"

"Deal."

Neil grabbed the colorful bar towel from Cal's shoulder, wiped his hands off, then shook my hand. "Good to see you, Chris."

"You too. I was sorry to hear about your apartment. I was there when firefighters were finishing up."

A new customer arrived and took a seat at the far end of the bar. Cal left to see what the newcomer wanted.

"Everything is gone but my old jalopy, plus some clothes I had in the trunk."

"Where were you when it happened?"

"Working. With the parade going on, it was a big day here. I normally wouldn't have been here for lunch on Saturday, but Cal asked me to come in. I need all the hours I can get."

"I'm glad you weren't in your apartment. Any idea what started it?"

"I hear rumors it was arson. Got a couple of ideas, but nothing to back them up."

"What—"

Charles magically appeared behind me before I could get Neil to share his ideas.

"Hey, Neil, Chris, sorry I'm late."

"Late for what?" Neil said.

Excellent question, I thought.

"Meeting Chris. Figured I'd beat him like I always do."

"Neil," Cal said from behind the bar. "My buddy over there wants a cheeseburger. Let's don't keep him waiting."

"I'd better get cookin'," he said as he smiled at his boss.

"Did I miss anything?" Charles said as Neil headed to the kitchen.

Cal handed Charles a Budweiser, another correct assumption by the bartender. He and I headed to a vacant table. The only other customers were the man at the bar plus the three undertaker look-alikes.

Brenda Lee's version of "Rockin' Around the Christmas Tree" serenaded us as we sat and took a sip of our drinks.

"You didn't say anything to Neil about what we wanted to talk to him about, did you?"

"No," I said. "He was busy, then you interrupted us when he was getting ready to tell me about the fire."

"Good," Charles said as Brenda finished singing. He pivoted toward the bar. "Hey, Cal, old buddy. Chris here wants to talk to Neil when he gets a chance."

"No problem, pard. I'll mosey in the kitchen, tell him to drop everything he's doing. Stop fixing food. Rush out here to take a meeting with two old-timers. Will that work?"

"Good plan, Cal," Charles said, skipping over Cal's sarcasm.

Luckily, Cal laughed as he headed to the kitchen.

Cal delivered the hamburger to the customer at the bar as Neil came our way.

Neil turned a chair around, sat, then put his elbows on the back of the seat. "Cal said two old geezers want to talk to me."

Charles looked around the room, then said, "Don't see any. Since you're here, Chris said you were going to tell him something about the fire."

"I did?"

"Neil, you said you'd heard it was arson, that you had a couple of ideas about who may've started it."

Roger Miller's "King of the Road" proved Cal hadn't replaced all his classic country songs with Christmas music.

Neil looked at the jukebox then at me. "I'm being paranoid. Probably doesn't have anything to do with what I'm thinking. No need to get into it."

"Tell us anyway," Charles said. There was a zero chance he'd let Neil off that easy.

"Remember when Cal hired me?"

"Sure," I said.

"He'd heard I'd been fired from the private security job in Charleston."

Charles interrupted, "Yeah, your boss at that toy factory fired you because you were being questioned by the cops about the bookie's murder."

Neil nodded. "Doing my civic duty and that jackass kicked me out. Pissed me off."

Charles said, "So?"

Charles, let the man talk, I thought. "Neil, go on."

"I'd worked there for four years. You learn a lot about a place when you're a night watchman. Get to snoop when no one's around. Lots of hours with nothing to do. It'd be hard to find a thief who'd want to break in a kid's toy manufacturing company. Anyway, I started piecing together some papers of the owner, Paul Davidson's his name, by the way. Anyway, he was mighty careless about leaving tax papers and P&L statements on his desk. I'm no accountant, hell, I'm just a dumb country boy, but it didn't take a number cruncher to figure there was a bunch of revenue Paul wasn't reporting to the IRS."

"How'd you figure it out?" Charles asked.

Neil smiled. "Didn't have to. All I did after he fired me was make a couple of calls to the IRS office in Charleston.

Guys, did you know they have a form you have to fill out to report fraud? They've got a form for everything." He shook his head. "Hell, I wasn't about to fill out a stupid form. I made the two calls, told them where and what, and if they wanted to catch a crook, they'd find him there. I wasn't going to do all the work for them."

"What happened?" Charles asked as if Neil wasn't going to tell us without being asked.

Cal hummed along with Charlie Rich's version of "Behind Closed Doors" as Neil took a sip of beer he'd brought with him to the table. No one else had entered the bar.

"One of the guys from the factory called a couple of weeks later, told me it was good I got out when I did." Neil laughed. "He didn't know I'd been fired. Said a group of suits swarmed all over the factory hauling out computers and everything from the file cabinets. My buddy wasn't sure what happened next, but Paul spent a lot of time talking to lawyers and storming around the factory looking like his head was going to explode. Best news I got in years."

"Neil," I said, "That's interesting. Sounds like he's getting what he deserves, but how's it related to the fire?"

"Suppose I left out an important part. Last week, my buddy at the factory called bitching about the extra work Paul was laying on him. He was always bitching about something. Anyway, he heard Paul telling one of his VPs he figured out who ratted him out to the Feds. Said he was going to get even with the SOB. Fellas, I'm that SOB."

I asked, "How would he have found out it was you?"

"Don't think he could. That's why I'm being paranoid. I didn't give the IRS my name. I never said anything at work hinting at me knowing about the business end of the company. Hell, I was just a dumb old night watchman."

Two customers arrived, sat at a table on the other side of the room, placed an order with Cal, who whistled for Neil, then pointed at the kitchen.

A subtle hint, it wasn't. Neil said he'd better do what Cal wanted. He didn't want to get fired from another job.

Ernest Tubb's version of "Blue Christmas" was playing, reminding everyone that Christmas was less than two weeks away.

Chapter Twelve

Charles and I went separate ways after leaving Cal's. The temperature had become uncharacteristically warm for this time of year. Adding the bright sunshine made it feel warmer, so I walked a few short blocks to Pewter Hardware to ask Larry how his sister-in-law and nephew were adjusting to their new residence. This was the store's busiest time of year, so I wasn't surprised there were vehicles overflowing the small, crushed-shell parking lot.

The interior of the tiny store was more crowded than the lot. Three customers waited in line at the check-out counter, four were blocking the narrow aisle near the seasonal decorations, while two others were flipping through a battery display.

Larry manned the register. He wore a velvet Santa's hat, but at five-foot-one, weighing a hundred pounds after a Thanksgiving meal, he looked more like one of Santa's elves. He was self-conscious about his diminutive size, so the elf comparison was one he'd not hear from me.

I wasn't surprised by the crowd but was surprised seeing Luke beside Larry bagging purchases. Brandon, Larry's only full-time employee was helping a customer carry three sacks to the door.

The customers who'd been waiting to check out completed their purchases and headed for the exit. Larry saw me standing out of the flow of customers, smiled, then put his arms around Luke. The nine-year-old was only a half-foot shorter than Larry, another observation I'd keep to myself.

"Chris, check out my new employee."

I smiled. "Have the child-labor police been in yet?"

"Hi, Mr. Landrum," Luke said, ignoring my comment. "Uncle Larry says I'm a big help."

"You look like you're doing a great job. You need to ask your uncle for a raise."

Luke chuckled. "Uncle Larry says I'm earning my rent, but I can leave whenever I want."

I started to comment when someone tapped my shoulder. I turned to see Rose standing behind me wearing an orange Pewter Hardware sweatshirt.

"Don't tell me Larry's put both of you to work."

"He's not that cruel. As you know, I'm short on clothes so Larry contributed this to the cause. Cindy and I are going to the mall tomorrow to rectify the situation."

"Rose," Larry said, "why don't you get some fresh air. Luke and I can hold down the fort."

She nodded then turned to me. "Up for a walk?"

"I can cram one in my schedule."

"Mom, don't worry about me. Uncle Larry needs me here."

Another customer was ready to check out, so Rose and I

left the store in the good hands of Larry, Luke, and, I suppose, Brandon.

"Which way?" Rose asked as we walked a block to Center Street.

"Have you been on the Folly Pier?"

"Luke and I started there once, but it was so cold we turned around. Today's nicer, I'm up for it if you are."

We walked six blocks to where Center Street dead-ends at the entrance to the Tides Hotel. Our walk was mostly silent, with Rose's only comments being about the illuminated sand dollar, dolphin, crab, and turtle decorations adorning light poles along the way. The Folly Beach Fishing Pier was adjacent to the Tides, so we turned at the hotel, before making our way up the long flight of steps to the pier's deck where a group of women were leaning against the railing watching the surf roll in. A middle-aged man was photographing two children sitting in a red chair big enough to hold someone the size of the Goodyear blimp.

"It's a lot warmer than the last time we were here. This is a great view of the beach."

I pointed to the far end of the thousand-foot-long structure. "It's even a better view from out there."

"What are we waiting for?" Rose said as she put her arm through mine and escorted me to the end of the pier.

When we reached the Atlantic end of the pier, we sat on a wooden picnic table and faced the shore. Rose was silent for a long time, before saying, "It's weird living in the house with Cindy."

"Were you close?"

I asked since Cindy had never mentioned a sister.

"Not really. With ten years between us, we had little in common. We have different fathers, you know."

"I didn't know. Cindy and I are good friends, but she seldom says anything about her life before moving to Folly."

Rose smiled. "That's no surprise. She's self-contained, irritatingly so at times."

I nodded.

"Her dad, Kenneth, was a coal miner near Evarts. That's in Harlan County, Eastern Kentucky. He'd dropped out of high school to work in the mines. Two years later, he married our mom, Ruth, then three years after that, Cindy came along."

"I thought she grew up in East Tennessee."

"Her dad didn't have much formal education, but was smart, or so mom said. She told me he realized if he kept working in the mines, his back would die before he did. He quit when Cindy was three. He'd heard about work in Tennessee from a friend who'd moved there a couple of years earlier. It was with the Sevier County Sheriff's Office. He packed up his family and moved to Kodak."

"Where you were born?"

She looked at the ocean for the longest time. I wasn't sure if she'd heard me. Finally, she said, "Three days shy of Kenneth's first anniversary with the Sheriff's Office, he pulled a man over for speeding. Nothing out of the ordinary. Nothing unusual until the man, later determined to be high on drugs, pulled a gun and shot Kenneth three times. He never had a chance. Cindy was four."

"That's horrible," I said, wondering if that's why Cindy seldom mentions her past.

"It got worse for Cindy. Five years later, Mom married a man named Boyd. He was a traveling shoe salesman, sold to small-town retail stores throughout the region. Mom was pregnant with me when they got married." She chuckled without a hint of humor then stared at the water. "Boyd told mom he could put up with one kid but not two. He left town, never to be heard from again." Cindy was Luke's age when I was born." She turned to me and smiled. "Cindy would kill me if she knew I was telling you."

"She won't hear it from me."

"Good. Not many years after that, Cindy graduated from high school. She had little interest in studying, but to keep mom happy, she moved in a dorm at the University of Tennessee, attended school off and on for three years before quitting. Instead of moving back to Kodak, she stayed in Knoxville. For eight years she bounced around dead-end jobs. She waited tables, tended bar, even sold encyclopedias door-to-door."

"She said she worked in law enforcement before moving here."

"She joined the same sheriff's office her dad was a member of. She never told me this, it's only amateur psycho-analyzing, but I think it was so her dad would've been proud of her following in his footsteps." She sighed. "Sure you won't tell her I told you?"

"You have my word."

She nodded. "Cindy said you were a pain in the ass but could be trusted. Otherwise, I wouldn't have said anything."

I laughed.

"While I'm spilling secrets, there's something else. I haven't told Cindy because I know her well enough to know if I did, she'd go all cop and blow it out of proportion."

"I can see that."

"The day before the apartment fire, my ex called. He was at the Crab Shack, wanted me to meet him."

"What'd you say?"

"Chris, I was shocked. I hadn't heard from him since I moved. He wanted to meet me without Luke. Probably shouldn't have, but I went. Told Luke I had to walk up the street for a few minutes and left him in the apartment. I felt bad about leaving him, but he was watching a monster movie and seemed okay." She turned to watch a large container ship lumber toward the entrance to the Charleston harbor.

I waited for her to continue.

"Lawrence, my ex, was sitting at a table acting smug. It's one of his more-practiced looks. He's a vice president at a Morristown bank, a job he got because his father is on the board. To put it mildly, I didn't greet him with open arms."

"What'd he want?"

"Us to come home—home to Morristown. Can you believe that? Mr. Hot Shot Bank Official got caught having an affair with a twenty-five-year-old teller at another bank. Now I'm supposed to come running back after the chick-adee dumped him."

"What'd you tell him?"

She surprised me with a laugh. "With two college degrees in English, I'd learned several ways to tell him to go, umm, have intercourse with himself. I used all of them, then cracked open a peanut and threw the shell at him."

I struggled to hold back a laugh, then said, "How'd he respond?"

"It wasn't the reaction he'd expected. His face turned red, his hands gripped his drink so hard, I was afraid he'd break the glass. He dropped a twenty on the table, stared at me, and whispered, "You'll regret it.""

"Think he started the fire?"

She shook her head. "No. That's why I haven't told Cindy."

"What makes you think he didn't?"

"Oh, I wouldn't have put it past him if it were only me. There's no way he would've endangered Luke, even if there was a minuscule chance his son would've been in the apartment. No way."

It may've been my imagination, but the wind picked up and my skin felt like the temperature dropped twenty degrees. I wish I had her confidence.

Chapter Thirteen

After walking Rose to Larry's store, my growling stomach reminded me I'd skipped two meals, a rare event. Instead of heading home, I stopped at Snapper Jack's, a large, multi-level restaurant on the corner of Ashley Avenue and Center Street. The restaurant is easy to give directions to since it faces the island's only traffic light. A college-age hostess in an aqua Snapper Jack's T-shirt escorted me to a table by a large window overlooking Center Street. In-season it would've been nearly impossible to get a table so quickly.

A server greeted me with a smile, a menu, an introduction, her name is Marcia and an inquiry about my drink choice. She headed to the bar once I said a glass of Cabernet. Since the restaurant had few customers, Marcia had my drink on the table before I could study the menu. She asked if I was ready to order. I begged for additional time, to which she said she'd be near the bar, for me to wave when I was ready.

Instead of studying the menu, I replayed what Rose shared about Cindy's background plus her revelation about her ex-husband's visit. I understood why she was confident he didn't set the fire, but I wasn't as understanding. It struck me as more than a coincidence he was on Folly fewer than twenty-four hours before the fire. Did he return to Tennessee after their meeting or stay in the area?

How could I find out? On a couple of instances when I wanted to know where someone had been staying, Chief LaMond provided invaluable assistance. Her title and charm were more than enough to get hotel desk clerks to check guest registers to see if the people she asked about had stayed in their facility. I'd told Rose I wouldn't share what she'd said with her sister, so asking Cindy was off the table. I knew an employee at the Tides who might be able to remember Rose's ex staying there, but it'd be a long shot.

I nearly dropped my drink, when someone said, "Thought that was you."

I turned to see Janice Raque standing by the table. "Oh, hi, Janice."

Janice is in her late fifties, five-foot-four, with short brown hair with patches of gray sneaking in. She wore an oversized, navy-blue sweatshirt, and black slacks. She also had a bottle of Lagunitas IPA in her hand.

"You're, umm, now don't tell me, you're Chris, right?" She swung the bottle in rhythm with her words.

"Good memory."

"Remember talking to you a couple of times in Hal's, umm, Cal's."

Janice had been a regular in Cal's when she was married. According to Cal, she and her husband often got in arguments until one of them stormed out.

She looked at the bar-height stool on the other side of the table. I took the hint.

"I'm having an early supper. Want to join me?"

"Supper from a wineglass?" She chuckled. "This is my supper." She held up the beer bottle.

Instead of answering my question, she pulled out the stool.

I handed her the menu. "I was getting ready to order. Want something to eat?"

"This is my third, maybe fourth beer. Suppose I'd better eat something to sop the hops." She laughed.

I began wondering if she'd underestimated the number of beers she'd consumed for supper. I motioned for Marcia. I ordered fish and chips and asked Janice if she knew what she wanted. She ordered a Folly salad. I wasn't sure what it was since I eat salad as often as I eat chocolate-covered oyster shells. Marcia asked if we needed more drinks. I hadn't finished my wine, so I declined. Janice didn't decline. I doubted a Folly salad would sop up enough hops to prevent Janice from falling off the stool.

After Marcia left, I said, "Janice, didn't you live in the apartment building that burned?"

"Damn, Chris, has a secret ever escaped from this island without being caught by a gaggle of people?"

"Someone was talking about the people displaced by the fire. Your name was mentioned. I remembered you from Cal's."

I left out the part about remembering her because she'd been a murder suspect.

"Yes, I'm one of the unlucky people who're now homeless."

"Found somewhere to stay?"

"Why? Want me to shack up with you?"

She definitely underestimated the number of beers she'd consumed.

I smiled. "Afraid I don't have room."

"Well crapola."

I was saved when Marcia deposited Janice's beer, then said our food would be out shortly. Janice had the new bottle to her lips before Marcia reached the kitchen. Now to move past Janice's comment about moving in.

"I was asking because I heard the Red Cross provided housing for the fire victims."

She held up two fingers. "Two nights, period. Did they think the apartment building would be rebuilt in two days?"

"Sorry."

"Oh well, that's water under the dam, or over the bridge, or, crap, whatever the saying is. I'm at the Holliday Inn a couple of weeks until I figure something out."

The Holliday Inn, not to be confused with the national hotel chain spelled with one "l," is a fourteen room, locally-owned hotel that's been around since the late 1940s. It's a block from the ocean, has reasonably priced rooms, and is one of only two hotels on the island.

"It's good you have somewhere to go."

"I suppose. Some are living in their cars."

"Did you know many of the others?"

"Not really. I've been there a little over a year. Ever since, umm, never mind. Anyway, I know Neil pretty well. Nice guy. He's been there as long as I have. I only know him from Cal's. He cooks there, you know. Seldom saw him around the apartment." She took another sip. "The young guy, the one with the red sports car, don't know his name for certain. Something like Sly."

"Ty," I interrupted.

"Okay, Ty. Anyway, that's all I know about him. Oh wait, he's got a cat."

"Lost," I said.

"Lost what?"

"His cat's named Lost."

"Damned stupid name for a cat."

I didn't disagree. "What about the African-American lady?"

Janice shook her head. "All I know is she nearly ran me down with her big-ass truck."

"What happened?"

"I got food at Bert's and was carrying it home. I got to our parking area when she whipped out of the lot, not looking where she was going. I was lucky or I wouldn't be here."

"Did she see you?"

"Said she didn't. She stopped, lowered her window, said she was sorry. It's no wonder she almost got me. It was dark, yet she had on these big sunglasses. Did she think she was a celebrity? Anyway, now you know all I know about her."

"What about the lady who moved in recently, the one with the young son?"

"She lived right under me. The kid kept the TV on loud. Thought about complaining. Knew it wouldn't do any good since the building was built cheap. Doubt there was a speck of insulation in it. Everyone could hear everything going on." Our meals arrived. Janice took a bite of salad, another sip of beer, then said, "That building was a fire waiting to happen. The damned landlord didn't fix anything. My bathroom sink leaked from the day I moved in. Suppose it don't leak no more." She laughed and took another drink. "Know what O'Leary, he's the landlord, was good at?"

"What?"

"Collecting rent. I could set my watch by the time he came knocking on the door the first of the month. I spilled the beans to everyone who asked me about renting there."

"Did many people ask?"

"A couple. The apartment on the first floor was vacant several months, so occasionally someone would see me outside and ask. Some guy, looked like a street person to me, asked. Told me he was Jeff, maybe Jerome. Anyway, he was looking for an apartment." She chuckled, took another sip of beer, then said, "Told him the apartment was fine unless the second floor fell on him. Chris, didn't know I was psychic, did you?"

I shook my head.

"Good ole Jeff or Jerome stopped asking me anything after that. Then one time I was telling a woman named Kinsey or Kaycee exactly what I thought. She thanked me."

"Where'd you meet her?"

"Opening my door, in fact, she followed me upstairs. She told me she owned a couple of rental units and had someone looking for a place to rent, but hers were full. She was a fast talker; said a bunch of other stuff I can't remember now. I gave her the full load about how O'Leary doesn't take care of my place. She turned and left, not as fast as Jeff or Jerome, but close. She said something about— Whoops!" Janice slipped off the chair. I grabbed her before she hit the floor.

"You okay?" I said, knowing she wasn't.

She giggled, then finished her beer. "Sure I can't shack up with you?"

"Afraid not," I said and became fascinated with my fish and chips, rather than looking her in the eye.

Marcia returned to ask if the food was okay and if we wanted something else to drink. I said I was fine. Fortunately, Janice said the same—for now.

"Janice, have any idea who may've started the fire?"

She took another sip, played with her napkin, while she looked out the window, then back to me. "Absolutely."

Not the answer I expected.

"Who?"

"My ex."

"Horace?"

"Absolutely."

"Why think it was him?"

"Don't think, know it was."

"How do you know?"

"You know he left me for a floozie in Mt. Pleasant."

"I'd heard you got a divorce. Didn't know the details."

"Left me with nothing except his dirty underwear. I had to move out of our nice condo in Mariner's Cay. I couldn't afford a two-bit ambulance-chasing lawyer to go after Horace for my share of what he had. Finally found one who'd do it on contingency." She chuckled. "He must've graduated last in his class. The poor fella was desperate to get a client. I told him Horace weren't no millionaire, but the shyster said he'd take the case anyway."

Interesting, I thought, but it didn't get me any closer to the reason Horace would've set the fire.

"Janice, why would Horace torch the building?"

"My attorney might not know how to get good-paying clients or have a fancy-schmancy office in downtown Charleston, but I'll tell you what he's good at. He's about driven Horace bananas harassing him for money, telling Horace's employer how much of a deadbeat his employee is."

I'll give it one more chance.

"Janice, why do you think Horace burned the building?"

"Chris, I don't know how many ways I can say it. It's as clear as day. Can't you see, he's pissed at me. Wants me to know it. Clear as day." She nodded like it was, well, clear as day, then took another drink.

It may be clear to her, although, in her current condition, I doubted anything was clear. I hadn't had four, maybe five, maybe no telling how many beers, but nothing she'd said led me to believe Horace had set the fire. Could he have? I suppose. Someone set it.

I made a couple more efforts to see if Janice could clarify how she "knew" her ex started the fire. I would've been more successful if I'd asked her to conjugate the verb imbibe in Hungarian. Then, I asked if she wanted me to walk her to her hotel. She declined and said she was moving to the bar and having one more for the road. Fortunately, her hotel was close, and she wouldn't be driving. As I walked away, she slurred one more effort to ask if she could shack up with me. I hoped she took my ignoring the question as no.

Chapter Fourteen

I had trouble sleeping; must've gone over today's conversations with the two fire victims a dozen times. Rose was certain her ex wouldn't have set the fire, but it still struck me as too great a coincidence that he was on Folly the day before the conflagration. He'd be near or at the top of my list of potential arsonists. On the other hand, Janice was certain her ex set it but provided nothing supporting her proclamation.

I attributed most of my sleeping problems to questions bouncing around in my head. It wasn't necessarily the questions that kept me awake, the lack of answers was my nemesis. Tonight, now this morning was the perfect example.

After three hours sleep, I decided a brisk walk in brisk weather to the Lost Dog Cafe would be good for my health. It would wake me up, provide me with a hearty breakfast, and allow my brain to find answers to the questions that'd kept me awake. Rationalizing was one of my strengths.

The restaurant was nearly full, so I was lucky to get one

of the small tables against the front wall. I was even luckier when Amber appeared, set a mug of coffee in front of me, then asked what she could do to make my day better. I told her if she joined me at the table, it would make my day better. She laughed and said she'd have to improve my day by serving, not joining me. I said I'd take what I could get. She must've been in a good mood because she asked if I wanted French toast rather than trying to get me to eat healthier. I said yes, she said she wondered why she wasted time asking.

Before breakfast arrived, Cindy LaMond arrived, saw me, then headed my direction.

"Going to invite me to join you?" she said, as she pulled up a chair, not waiting on an answer.

I said, "You're always welcome to join me, Chief."

"Weren't you getting ready to ask if you could buy me breakfast?"

"Of course, I was," I said, not seeing a wise alternative.

Amber was quick to the table with coffee for Cindy, who smiled at the server, and said, "I'll have what he's having."

Amber returned the smile, and said, "How do you know—"

"French toast?"

Amber chuckled then headed to put in Cindy's order.

Cindy blew across the mug then cautiously took a sip, before saying, "I hear you sauntered to the end of the pier with my younger sister while she deserted her poor son stuck doing manual labor for a slave driver at a local hardware store."

"It's no wonder why you're Chief. You know everything that happens on your six-mile-long, half-mile-wide slice of earth."

"It helps that my confidential informant is a lad of nine who spent two hours last night gushing about how much fun he had at his uncle's store, while his mother gushed, not for two hours, but nevertheless gushed about how great it was talking to an adult without her son hearing every word. The only thing I disagreed with was her calling you an adult. I let her stay in her fantasy world and didn't tell her about the true you."

"Kind of you."

"She was too happy for me to ruin her mood. I wish she could be that happy all the time. Since the divorce, she's been having migraines, bouts of depression, and in general, miserable."

"She was in a good mood yesterday."

"She's coming out of it some. I'm afraid her moods are affecting Luke. Rose tries to shield him from everything bad, but he's perceptive."

"It's been rough on her, plus the fire didn't help. Time will take care of many of the bad moods."

"I hope you're right Psychiatrist Chris." Cindy took another sip as Amber arrived with our matching breakfasts.

We each focused for a moment on food, before I said, "Learn anything new about the fire?"

"Like who set it?"

"That'd be informative."

She rolled her eyes. "If only that easy. I did learn something interesting about the landlord, Russell O'Leary." She took another bite.

I waited for her to continue, hoping I wouldn't have to ask what. I was pleased she was more open to talking about it than she'd been when she accused me of butting into her business the first time I asked about O'Leary.

She finally continued, "Don't you want to know what?"

"Chief, what'd you learn?"

"That's better. For starters, Mr. O'Leary is three months behind on the building's mortgage."

"Was it well-insured?"

"Excellent question, motive-detector Chris. Mr. O'Leary is not only a landlord, he's psychic. Two months ago, he increased coverage on the building."

"Making him a candidate for arsonist of the year."

"If you weren't so old, so very very old, I'd put you on the force."

She could've left out the *very very* part, but I'll let it go. "What else?"

"What else what?"

"When you mentioned he was three months behind on his mortgage, you said, 'For starters,' so what else did you learn?"

"Chris, I wish you'd stop listening to everything I say."

I shrugged.

She took a bite of French toast, then a sip of coffee before continuing, "Remember I told you he said he was in Atlanta at some get-rich seminar the day of the fire?"

"I remember. Did you already forget I listen to everything you say?"

"Smartass."

I smiled.

"He said the seminar was at the Westin Peachtree Plaza in downtown Atlanta. Said he didn't stay there because it cost too much. He claimed to have stayed at a nearby cheaper hotel he—surprise, surprise—can't remember the name of. Before you ask, he said he paid cash so there wouldn't be a record of him staying there even if he could remember the name."

"He would've registered under his name; probably showed ID even if he paid cash."

"Probably, but know how many hotels there are in Atlanta? Besides, his entire story sounds off."

"Sounds fishy, doesn't it?"

"Ya think?"

"I do. Now what?"

"I finish my breakfast, cuss myself all the way back to the office for eating more calories than the total one-day consumption of everyone combined in a small, farming community in Tanzania, then close my office door so I can take a nap."

"I was thinking more about what you're going to do about Russell O'Leary."

"Hell if I know."

"Sounds like a plan."

Chapter Fifteen

While Cindy and I didn't solve who set the fire, or for that matter, didn't solve anything other than hunger, she said her plan was to learn more about Russell O'Leary's financial situation. I said my plan was to take a nap. She told me she was jealous.

Charles was parked on my front step when I got home. His 1961 Schwinn bicycle leaned against my screened-in porch. He wore a royal blue and white sweatshirt with Sierra Nevada College under the outline of an eagle on the front, his Tilley, and in a touch of irony, tan khaki work pants, an activity he hadn't participated in for decades.

"You're not home," he said as he pointed over his shoulder at the door.

"Am now. Did you run out of places to hang out?"

"Thought if we're going to catch whoever torched the building, we should talk."

"Who said we were going to catch the arsonist?"

"Me. Didn't you hear me?"

Arguing with Charles is like arguing with a clump of seaweed.

"Want to come in where we can talk in a warm room?"

"Why do you think I'm here?"

I started to open the door, when Charles grabbed my arm, tilted his head toward Bert's Market.

"Isn't that Ty?"

The young man was standing at the corner of the building talking to a man I knew to be homeless. "Yes."

Charles pulled me toward the store. "Look, he wants to talk to us."

I wasn't certain how Ty's talking to a homeless man meant he wanted to talk to us, but I was interested in asking if he'd heard anything new about the fire.

Ty saw us coming, told the man he had to go, then greeted Charles and me with a smile.

"Hey, Charles, you're big into animals. Want to meet Lost?"

"You bet."

Ty grinned like he was going to show Charles the Hope diamond. The Miata was tucked in the back of the small, sandy lot. The car was parked next to a dilapidated sailboat that looked like it hadn't been in the water since the flood that took Noah and his boat for a ride.

The feline's proud papa unlocked the passenger door. It opened to the scraping sound of metal against metal, followed by a meow loud enough to have come from a wild-cat. The grey kitten he lifted out of the car didn't look like it could've made such a loud noise, but it was the vehicle's only occupant.

"Meet Lost," Ty said as he handed Charles the kitten.

"Wow," Charles said, "a polydactyl."

That sounded like some sort of a dinosaur.

I said, "A what?"

Charles shook his head like he was having to teach a robin how to catch worms.

"Chris, you never cease to amaze me." He pointed Lost at me then lifted the kitten's leg in my direction. "Polydactyl. A furry little critter with six toes on one or more of its paws. See?"

The front right paw did have six toes. "Oh," I said, indicating I didn't have a future as a veterinarian.

"Ernest Hemingway became a big fan after someone gave him a white one. He named it Snow White. Today there are about fifty descendants of his cats at his former house in Key West."

"Half are polydactyl," Ty added, further reinforcing my ignorance.

Charles had run out of trivia, so he turned to Ty and asked how he got Lost, more importantly, how he'd come up with the name.

Ty proceeded to share the same story he'd told me about coming to Folly on vacation, seeing a girl named Aimee, staying here while his friends returned to Baltimore, getting the job at Bert's. That was as far as he got when he was telling me the first time he'd talked about her, so I began paying closer attention.

Charles suggested we move out of the shadows of the large trees on two sides of the lot and move to where the sun was peeking through so we could stay warm. Ty and I followed him to the side of the dumpster where Charles leaned on the large, industrial-sized waste container, petting Lost the entire time.

"After Aimee and I talked a few times, I wanted to give

her something. You know, something to bond our love."

Charles said, "Love?"

Ty lowered his head. "Well, not love exactly. I liked her. A guy I met in the store told me he had three kittens he was trying to find homes. I went to see them. Lo and behold, this little one was the cutest. Just seeing it made me think of Aimee. How could I not take it? Gave it to Aimee a few days later." He stopped, shook his head, then continued, "Fellas, how could I know she was allergic to cats?"

"That's too bad," Charles said.

"That wasn't the baddest part," Ty said. "She was engaged. She didn't have a diamond ring on her finger, so how was I to know?"

Charles repeated, "That's too bad."

"You can say that again. I figured I could overcome the fiancée, but not the cat allergy. That's how I ended up with this little one. Also, how it got its name. I got the cat, lost the girl, so I named it Lost."

Charles said, "Sounds like the right name."

I thought it would've been a much shorter story if he'd named it Six Toes.

I realized we'd been standing outside for a fairly long time. So, I said, "Ty, are we keeping you from work?"

"No, I'm off. I worked most of the night. Going to head to the Walmart parking lot so I can curl up in the car to get some sleep."

Charles handed Lost back to Ty, then said, "Before you go, have any idea who burned your building?"

Unlike many people who talk to Charles, Ty didn't appear thrown by the change of directions

"Wish I knew. If I did, I'd make him sleep in my car a

few nights. That's punishment for putting all of us out of our homes."

Charles nodded. "So, no idea?"

"Not for certain, but if I was a betting man, I'd put a few bucks on Nick Matthews."

"Who's he?" I asked.

"Aimee's fiancée."

Charles said, "Why him?"

Lost began meowing so Ty put him back in the car, said he'd be with him in a minute, then scraped his feet on the sandy parking lot surface. "Well, you know how I said I figured I could overcome the fiancée but not Aimee's allergy?"

Charles nodded.

"Well, I didn't give up easily. I think Aimee told Nick how I was showing interest. I heard he had a temper, beat up another guy who'd been sniffing around his gal. Now, he never said anything to me at first, but I saw him in the store a few times after Aimee quit to take a waitressing job at Planet Follywood. He gave me the evil eye. The last time I saw him, he walked close to where I was stocking the bread shelf, and said something like, "You'll get yours.""

Charles said, "You think he torched your building because of that comment?"

"Like I said, I'd put money on it, on it. Not a lot, though."

Ty yawned and Lost made a moaning sound from the car. I figured our conversation was over. I thanked him for telling us about Lost.

Chapter Sixteen

Charles had to deliver a wetsuit from the surf shop to a man from Seattle renting a house on West Ashley Avenue. We walked to my house where he straddled his bike, pedaled off, leaving me standing in the yard realizing I had nowhere to be, nor anything to do. After spending what seemed like a zillion years experiencing the daily grind working in a large healthcare company, it was a good feeling. Something else that made me feel good was spending time with Barbara Deanelli, owner of Barb's Books, a small, used bookstore on Center Street. We've dated for a couple of years. I hadn't seen her in more than a week, so it was time to rectify that situation. While Charles was delivering a wetsuit, I could get some much-needed exercise walking to her store. The bookstore was housed in the same space that had previously been Landrum Gallery, a photo gallery I'd owned until it became clear that losing thousands of dollars a year wasn't the wisest use of my limited retirement savings. Residents and vacationers could live without my photographic prints, so I swallowed my pride and closed the business.

Two customers were browsing rows of books as I entered. Barb had strung multi-colored Christmas lights across the top of the shelves facing the entry. On a small table at the front of one of the aisles, she'd arranged books with colorful dust jackets in a shape intended to resemble a Christmas tree. Three boxes the size that'd hold jewelry were wrapped and set beside the book tree. It looked more like a pyramid-shaped pile of books than a Christmas tree, but I'd keep that observation to myself. The store's decorations fell far short of Cal's display, but the overall impression should put visitors in the spirit of the season.

One of the customers moved to the counter and handed Barb a credit card. Barb was in her mid-sixties, looked younger, stood my height at five-foot-ten, but much thinner. She had short black hair, hazel eyes, and a captivating smile currently being used on her customer.

She didn't notice me standing in the entry until she'd finished bagging the purchase. She used another of her captivating smiles on me. The remaining customer was still flipping through books, so Barb came around to me, gave me a kiss on the cheek, pointed to the door leading to the small office in the back of the store, then asked if I wanted coffee. I nodded. She said for me to fix each of us one, that she'd join me once the customer leaves.

When I'd had a business in the space, the room she called her office served more as a hangout for my friends, where a few of us could goof off, sip on a beverage, and discuss the latest happenings on the island. In other words, share gossip and good company. Barb had transformed the space to look more like a law office rather than a backroom in a retail business. She'd been a successful attorney in Pennsylvania before moving to Folly, so the law office motif was understandable.

I brewed two mugs of coffee in the Keurig, then settled in a comfortable chrome and black leather chair to wait. I began thinking of what Ty shared about who he thought started the fire. I didn't know anything about Aimee's fiancée other than what Ty had said, so I had no way of knowing if he was capable of such a drastic move to, umm, to what? Was the fire intended to harm Ty? If so, wouldn't the boyfriend have been able to see if Ty was working when he started it? If he only wanted to scare Ty away from Aimee, was he evil or reckless enough to burn a building, possibly harming other residents? Did Nick even make the comment Ty thought he'd made, or was Ty's imagination or guilt over trying to steal Nick's fiancée working overtime?

"Chris, are you asleep, or is your head somewhere else?" Barb said.

She was reaching for the coffee.

"Sorry, guess I was daydreaming."

Seasonal sounds from the Trans-Siberian Orchestra flowed from a Bose sound system on the desk.

"Were visions of sugar plums dancing in your head?" she asked, as she rolled her desk chair closer to the door so she could see if anyone entered the store.

I didn't know what a sugar plum was but didn't share my ignorance. "Nothing that jolly. How's business?"

"Excellent. I'm surprised. There aren't many vacationers this time of year, but the locals have been fantastic. Seems there's an uptick in book sales, not only here, but in stores everywhere."

That wasn't something I ever said about photographs when I had the gallery.

"Fantastic. Thought I'd stop to see if you wanted to grab supper this evening."

She smiled. "Thought you'd never ask."

We set a time and location, then she said, "I suppose you heard about the fire out past your house."

"Charles and I walked out there while they were fighting it."

"You chose a fire over the Christmas Parade. I'm shocked." She laughed, then added, "Not."

"We figured it was big when we saw Santa kicked off the fire engine."

"Did you know any of the residents?"

"I knew three before the fire. Didn't know them well but had talked with each a few times."

Barb's eyes narrowed as she stared at me. "Three before the fire. Now how many do you know?"

I told her about meeting Rose Wheeler, her son Luke, and their relationship to Chief LaMond.

"One of my customers told me yesterday the Chief had a sister and her apartment was in the building. Did you know about the sister before meeting her?"

"No, Cindy doesn't share much about her past."

Barb agreed then said, "Do you know Noelle Ward?"

I was surprised she mentioned the name. "Met her in the apartment's parking lot after the fire. Why?"

"She's one of my better customers. Came in a few times when she moved here, but in the last few months, she's been in several times a week. If you've talked to her, you probably know she's writing a novel. She's bought several mysteries, says for research." Barb chuckled. "First time in, she was in the mystery section, then noticed me nearby. She looked at me, or I think she did, I couldn't tell for sure since she had on sunglasses. She looked in my direction and said, I remember it almost verbatim, 'One day my book will be right here, someone will've read it, sold it to you, to be read again.' She seemed both confident and naïve at the same time. I like that gal."

"She told me she was writing a novel but didn't say much about it other than it's set on an island like Folly. The main character is a female private detective."

"I'm surprised she said that much. She's not loquacious. I haven't seen her since the fire."

"She's living out of her truck, so I imagine she has a lot on her mind."

"That's too bad. Have the others found places to live?"

"Rose and her son have temporarily moved in with Cindy and Larry. Janice Raque is staying at the Holliday Inn. I don't think the others have found anything."

Barb took a sip of coffee, then said, "What about Hope House?"

"It's full. I talked to Burl the day after the fire. He's looking for other options."

"That's too bad. I hear it was arson. Does Cindy know who set it?"

"Not that I've heard."

"You mean you're not pestering her daily to find out what she knows?"

"Why would you say that?"

She looked in her coffee mug, then smiled. "Because that's what you do."

"She doesn't know," I said. "It started in a vacant apartment on the first floor, so there's no way of knowing intent."

"I suppose she's taking a hard look at the landlord. That's where I'd start."

"Cindy's checking. Do you know him?"

"What's his name?"

"Russell O'Leary."

"Doesn't ring a bell. What's his financial situation?"

"Three months behind on the mortgage. Spends near nothing on maintenance."

"In my other life, our firm represented a guy accused of torching his five-story office building."

"Did he do it?"

"Jury didn't think so."

"What did you think?"

"My gut said he did, but like a good defense attorney, I never asked. He had more debt than Portugal. Are you and Charles trying to find out?"

"We're more interested in helping the displaced residents find housing."

"Good. Arsonists are dangerous. They can look like anyone, can be part of society like everyone else. In other words, they don't look or act like crooks, don't wave guns around announcing their intentions."

"I'll keep that in mind."

"Any luck finding living arrangements for the displaced residents?"

I shook my head.

Barb jumped up from the chair, said she was needed in front, but before she left, said, "Chris, I have faith you'll be able to help them."

I wish I shared her confidence.

Chapter Seventeen

It was four hours before I was to meet Barb. The unseasonably warm weather was still hanging around, so I decided to continue my off and on effort to walk wherever I needed to go around town. One of the New Year resolutions I'd been considering was to eat healthier combined with exercise, which in my dictionary meant walking, not other activities they torture people with in gyms. Why wait until January to begin?

I walked across the bridge heading off Folly then continued past where Center Street morphs into Folly Road. I turned on Mariner's Cay Drive and past the guardhouse with a gate that'd keep out unauthorized vehicles but did nothing to stop foot traffic. Over the years, I had known a few people who lived in Mariner's Cay, including Janice Raque. The large development consisted of a handful of residential buildings plus a marina. Several condos displayed colorful strands of Christmas lights around the perimeter of the screened-in patios, and on three balconies there were popular blow-up cartoon characters wearing Santa hats. I didn't walk through the development often, but it provided a different view than I was used to on my wanders around Folly.

I leaned against the rail on the walkway to the marina to watch several docked mid-size boats gently sway to the movement of the Folly River. I didn't know which building Janice had lived in or if they had a boat but being here gave me a chance to think more about her theory that Horace started the fire. I'd seen Horace a couple of times when they'd been in Cal's but had never spoken to him. From what I'd heard, he and Janice were in a rocky relationship. They'd often argue while at Cal's so I could only imagine how they'd gotten along in the privacy of their condo. Janice had a temper and according to an acquaintance who's a member of the Folly Beach City Council, she attended council meetings and wasn't shy about sharing opinions. What I didn't know was if Horace had built enough resentment to burn her building, nor did any significant revelations come to me as I watched the water flow by.

I crossed the bridge on my return to Folly then detoured on my walk home to stop by the Post Office to pick up what normally consisted of a "once in a lifetime" opportunity to get hearing aids at "unbelievable" low prices, a chance to consolidate all my credit cards into one so I could save thousands of dollars a year, or countless other "fantastic" offers for senior citizens.

I deposited the two "amazing" offers *du jour* in the trash receptacle the Post Office wisely placed near the exit. I thought about walking next door to Pewter Hardware to see Larry but rejected the idea after noticing his lot full and spaces along the road filled with vehicles. Cindy wasn't kidding when she said this was his busiest time of year.

Across the street, on a hill that led to the Folly River Park, Noelle Ward was seated in the shade. She was staring at her phone pointed toward the Post Office. At least, I assumed that's where her eyes were directed since I couldn't tell for sure. She wore her oversized sunglasses, a black sweatshirt, black jeans, and a dark gray jacket. I waved and she gave a tentative return wave as I walked over.

"Planning on robbing the Post Office?" I said, hoping to solicit a smile.

"They don't carry enough cash," she said, then laughed.

"Good point. I'm Chris, by the way. What brings you out here?"

She looked around, stood, and brushed off the back of her jeans. "I remember your name from the other day. I'm Noelle. It's getting cool in the shade. Want to move up there in the sun?"

"Lead on," I said.

She moved to the edge of the street, then fifty or so yards toward Center Street, before following the paved footpath into the park. The center of the small park was in full sun, so we sat at one of the picnic tables overlooking the city's Christmas tree.

She stretched her arms over her head, then turned to me. "Bet you're wondering what I was doing back there?"

"It crossed my mind."

"When we met, I told you I was writing a novel. Want to hear what it's about?"

That didn't answer why she was staring at the Post Office, but I was curious about her book. "Sure. You said it was a murder mystery. You were living here for research."

She smiled. "Good memory for someone who doesn't read."

I was surprised she remembered, especially since I told her while we were staring at her burned-out apartment building.

"You're the first author I've met, so I'm intrigued."

"My protagonist is a thirty-year-old, single, African-American female who's a fledgling private detective in a small, predominantly white town in Georgia."

"Sounds a lot like someone I know."

"Except for the private detective and Georgia part."

"Suppose that's why it's a novel and not non-fiction."

She smiled, which I was beginning to see as one of her most attractive and often-used traits.

"Shonda Black, the protagonist, opened a detective agency several months earlier and hasn't attracted any clients. She's depressed, on the verge of giving up, when a fifteen-year-old black teenager walks into her office. He came to her because she's the only black private eye in town." She hesitated, then said, "Let me back up a little. There'd been a bank robbery a week earlier in the next town over. Now to the kid walking in. He tells Shonda he saw the robbers in town when they were in a small grocery. It's a lot like Bert's Market. The boy, I call him Gabriel, tells Shonda he went to the police about seeing the bad guys. They laughed at him, told him he was seeing things, that the robbers had fled the state. That was why he was at her door. As you can probably guess, Gabriel doesn't have money to pay Shonda. She figured if she could catch the robbers the publicity would attract clients, the paying kind. I don't need to tell you more for you to guess Shonda catches the robbers. The end. My dream, only a dream at this point, is to make it the first book in a Shonda Black Mystery Series."

"That's great, Noelle."

"Thank you. Now all I need to do is finish writing it, write the second book in the series, and collect my Nobel Prize in Literature." She laughed and tapped my leg.

I laughed with her, then said, "Is a Post Office in your book?"

"Sorry, I drifted a little from telling you what I was doing."

"It was interesting."

"Interesting enough for you to read it when it comes out?"

"I'll not only read it, I'll write a letter to the Nobel Prize committee telling them they could stop looking. Your book is the winner."

She chuckled. "You make up stuff better than I do."

"The Post Office?"

"Research. Like I told you, the city where Shonda Black works is like Folly Beach. Small town, beach community, full of quirky characters. Most small towns are populated by people who are more similar than different, but I grew up in Missouri, no ocean nearby. Up until I decided to write the next Great American Novel, I wasn't good at observing people, how they dress, how they act, how they talk. I moved into the apartment that's now charcoal because it's like the place Shonda lives. Heck, I even bought the Dodge Ram 1500 pickup because it seemed like the kind Shonda would drive."

"You were researching people leaving the Post Office?"

"Yes. I've spent most every hour I'm not working watching people. Watching how they eat, how close they sit to each other, how some lean over when talking to someone else, how others speak loud not caring if their voice irritates others around them. I'm studying how they shop, how they move over so others can pass them in aisles, or on the sidewalks, all sorts of scenarios." She held up her phone. "I'm also taking videos so I can study people later."

"You're taking this seriously."

"I'm good at my day job, enjoy writing ad copy. If I want to be a good novelist, I have to study all phases of the process. One thing we do in the ad agency is to use focus groups to observe how people react to our various ads. For lack of better terms, Folly Beach is my large focus group."

"I'm not the person to ask about writing a novel, but it appears you know what you need to do."

"Time will tell, Chris."

"Changing the subject, have you found somewhere to live?"

"My Dodge condo."

"I was thinking somewhere without wheels."

"Not yet. I'm making the most of it. Think I'll add that Shonda's apartment gets burned by the bank robbers, so she has to live in her truck."

"That's turning lemons into lemonade."

She laughed, "Hmm, turning lemons into lemonade. I need to put that in an ad someday." She turned serious. "Did I give you my number the other day?"

I patted my phone. "Right here."

"Living in a truck is good for research, not so good for my back. You'll let me know if you hear of any apartments?"

"Absolutely."

She started to rise.

"Noelle, one more thing. When we met and were talking about the fire, you said something about being warned. What'd you mean?"

"Oh, it was nothing."

She'd already used that line on me. Time to press. Charles would be proud of me.

"Noelle, it wasn't nothing or you wouldn't have said it. Please tell me what you meant?"

Her hand gripped the bottom of the picnic table's seat. I was afraid she wasn't going to respond until she said, "Two weeks before the fire, I found a note under the windshield wiper. It was printed on that kind of paper with all the little squares."

"Graph paper?"

"Yeah. It said, this is paraphrasing, if you know what's good for you, you'll pack up and get off Folly."

"Was that all?"

"Yes."

"You have an idea who it may've been from?"

"Wish I did."

"Had you angered anyone?"

"Not that I know of." She removed her sunglasses and squeezed the bridge of her nose. "Not anyone."

"Any ideas?"

"My first thought was someone put it there by mistake. It's not the only black Dodge Ram in town."

"Why did you change your mind?"

"Mine's the only truck like it at the apartment or at nearby houses. How could someone get it confused? I then thought it could've been from someone who saw me nosing around, watching people, shooting video. They could've been doing something wrong and thought I caught them.

Something like that. Or it simply could've been someone who doesn't like black folk."

"Do you still have the note?"

She shook her head then shrugged. "It was in the apartment."

"Did you tell the police?"

"No. It'd be like Gabriel in my book going to the police. Nothing could be learned from a note on a piece of scrap paper. Unlike Gabriel, I'm trying to forget it."

"Do you think the person who left it started the fire?"

She stood a second time. "Chris, I don't know what to think," she hesitated, then added, "these are nice Christmas decorations."

That appeared to be her way of ending talk about the note. "They are nice."

"I'd better be going," she said, reached out and shook my hand. "Nice talking to you."

I agreed with her.

She left leaving me with more questions than when I arrived.

Chapter Eighteen

Barb and I were to meet at Wiki Wiki Sandbar, one of Folly's newest, and undoubtedly largest restaurants, located a block from my cottage. I was standing outside the multi-level, tiki-themed restaurant ten minutes before our scheduled rendezvous. Barb, unlike Charles who considered thirty-minutes early to be on time, arrived five minutes later. She wore a lightweight tan jacket over a red blouse, black slacks, and a smile that brightened the early-evening darkness.

"Been waiting long?" she said then kissed my cheek.

"A couple of minutes. Hungry?"

She put her arm behind my back and nudged me toward the entry. "Starved. This is my first time here. How about you?"

"Once, but only to the bar. It's interesting."

She pointed to the other side of the L shaped structure. "One of my customers told me the style is mid-century modern, said there are five distinct rooms."

Before I could get a more-detailed architectural description of the building, a bubbly hostess escorted us to what she called the Wave Room where we were seated under a sculpture featuring hundreds of glass balls anchored to the ceiling. We were handed menus and told Karen would be our server.

I looked around the modern-looking room, mid-century or otherwise, while Barb focused on the menu. As promised, Karen appeared at the table before I'd finished gazing around the room. She asked if we wanted something to drink. Barb, who'd already studied the drink choices, said she'd have an Aloha from the Edge, which a quick peek at the menu told me was vodka and passionfruit. I didn't want Barb to have to wait while I agonized over the menu trying to figure out what each drink was, so I said a glass of Cabernet. Karen headed to the bar while Barb continued studying the menu. I envied her metabolism. She could eat like a sumo wrestler yet never gain an ounce. She pointed at my menu and told me to stop looking around and decide what to order.

The server returned with our drinks as I made my decision, thank goodness. Barb ordered a Korean short rib, I went with the pork ribs, mainly because I was more familiar with the ribs than some of the other items.

With the pressure of ordering at a new restaurant out of the way, Barb asked what I'd been doing since I left the store earlier today. She added, what I was doing while she was hard at work.

I told her about my chance meeting with Noelle and what she'd said about the note on her truck.

"Think she was clueless about who put it there or why?"

I nodded. "Sounded convincing. I had to push to get her

to tell me about it. I don't know if she was worried about it or thought it was so inconsequential it wasn't important enough to mention."

"Next time she's in, I'll see if I can get her to talk about it. Does she know we're dating?"

"Don't know. Why?"

"If she does, it'd give me a better entrée into the discussion about the note since you could've shared the information with me."

"True."

This was the first time Barb hadn't tried to discourage me from getting involved in something that clearly was none of my business, something best left to the police. I wanted to point out the historic moment but thought it wouldn't be wise, besides, Karen was at the table with our food. Little could keep my companion from grabbing a fork and digging in.

A few bites later, I said, "If you get a chance, check with some of your customers to see if they know of an apartment for Noelle. She's looking for what she calls a dump, something in line with where she was. She wants to stay in character with the protagonist in her novel."

Barb smiled. "So, you want me to ask customers if they know a dump for rent?"

"You could say it more lawyerly, something like a budget-priced rental unit."

Two bites later, she said, "Did Noelle think the fire was set because she didn't take the note's advice?"

"She didn't say. It seems more than a coincidence, although from what I've heard, she's not the only resident who'd upset someone enough to set the fire."

"Chris, remember I told you I defended an arsonist in my previous life?"

"Yes."

"To give him a proper defense, I researched arsonists. The consensus of experts profiled most as young males."

"That narrows it down to a few hundred folks over here."

"Chris, there's more, if you'll let me finish."

"Please do," I said before taking a sip of wine.

"In addition to being young guys, more than seventy-five percent were Caucasian."

I wanted to say that didn't eliminate many of Folly's young males. A dollop of wisdom made me nod instead of speaking.

"They also score relatively low on intelligence tests."

"Did that profile help with your client?"

"Sort of."

"Meaning?"

"He's Caucasian, a graduate of one of the nation's top business schools, plus, is in his late fifties. The profile of an arsonist typically refers to a serial arsonist, someone who's obsessed with starting fires. My client was accused of being a one-off arsonist. He allegedly set the fire for money, not kicks. There was no history of him starting others."

"So how did the profile sort of help in his defense?"

"Reasonable doubt. If I cluttered the defense with other possibilities, regardless of how remote, jurors' minds could be influenced."

"Were they?"

"I told you, he was found not guilty."

I smiled. "Not necessarily innocent."

She returned the smile.

"How does this relate to the apartment fire?"

"Are the police looking for a serial arsonist or someone who set the fire for a reason other than seeing a massive fire? Have there been other unexplained fires on Folly or in the area in recent days, weeks, months?"

"If there've been others, the apartment fire may've had nothing to do with Noelle or other residents. The motivation of the person starting it was to create a fire."

"You're catching on. Want dessert?"

A change of subject, a hint. Barb was motioning for the server before I could say yes.

Dessert was ordered, which led to more pleasant discussions, overall, a pleasant evening. On my way home after escorting Barb to her condo, I decided to call Chief LaMond in the morning to ask if she had any update on the fire. Additionally, I could ask if she was aware of other recent unsolved fires.

Chapter Nineteen

The Chief answered with, "Good morning, Chief LaMond speaking. How may I be of assistance?"

Her salutation couldn't have been clearer than if she'd said, "I can't talk. If you don't hang up, I'll have you arrested for pissing me off."

"Call when you get a chance."

"Of course."

I didn't expect to hear from her soon, so in quest of healthy exercise, I walked next door to Bert's for a heart-unhealthy cinnamon Danish plus coffee. I didn't realize until I was out the door that the weather had tanked overnight. The unseasonably warm December temperatures were gone, replaced by what must've been the mid-forties. To someone from the North, it would've felt mild, but to Lowcountry residents, it felt like the deep freeze. It was easier to keep heading to the store than return home for a jacket. In addition to getting breakfast, I also wanted to see how Ty was doing.

I succeeded in getting the Danish and coffee, but Ty was nowhere to be seen. According to Caroline, another of Bert's helpful employees, Ty had the day off.

I was heading to the register, then home to eat my Danish in peace, when I heard a familiar voice coming from behind the nearby shelf.

"Morning, Mr. Photo Man. I see you're eating healthy as usual."

It's been a while since Charles greeted me with the Mr. Photo Man moniker. On a strange level, it was refreshing to hear. He wore a heavy gold sweatshirt with Wyoming Cowboys in brown letters on the front. No, I wasn't going to ask about the sweatshirt.

"Got to keep my energy level up," I said, "What're you doing on this side of town?"

Charles lived about seven blocks past Bert's but seldom frequented the store.

"Exercise. Teddy Roosevelt said, 'Let us rather run the risk of wearing out than rusting out.'"

Another of Charles's quirks is quoting United States Presidents. He says reading what they said keeps his mind active. I've attributed it to him wanting to be different, something he was without quoting anyone.

"There's little chance of you rusting." His hands were empty, so I added, "You getting something or working on wearing out."

"Out for a walk, but now that I see you, let me tell you about a brilliant idea I had in the middle of the night."

"Tell me, then I'll decide if it's brilliant."

"I'll go with you to your house where you can leave your breakfast, then we can saunter around town while you're listening to my brilliant idea."

I had nothing better to do, besides, I could get a jacket if we were going to saunter around. Charles said he'd get coffee while I paid. Five minutes later, I'd upgraded my wardrobe, took a bite of Danish, then headed toward the Folly Pier with my friend.

I was beginning to question the wisdom of walking on the pier. The stiff ocean breeze made it feel colder than the upper-forties. Why couldn't Charles tell me his brilliant idea in a restaurant or my cottage? We'd walked halfway to the end of the pier, when he said, "Got another idea."

"Is it as brilliant as the one you haven't shared yet?"

"Brilliant, no. Warmer, yes. Why don't we go to the hotel's lobby?"

I didn't know what his other idea was, but to my shivering body, his latest sounded brilliant.

Christmas decorations were scattered throughout the lobby of the oceanfront hotel. Jay, a friend who's worked at the hotel for years, greeted us with, "Merry Christmas, gentlemen. You two spreading tidings of comfort and joy?"

"Always," Charles said.

I wasn't as confident, so I shook Jay's hand and said it was nice seeing him before telling him we were getting out of the cold.

"You're always welcome here. Let me know if there's anything you need," Jay said and left us in the seating area off the lobby.

"Okay, Charles, let's hear your idea."

He warmed his hands by rubbing them together, gazed around the empty area, then said, "Brilliant idea. Ty has a cat, cute little thing." He stopped and nodded.

"Yes."

"Who else do you know with a cat?"

I wasn't ready for a quiz and took too long to answer.

"Well, who?"

"I've got it. Good old Mr. Sarnaw. He used to walk that big black cat with a leash down the sidewalk. First time I'd seen someone walking a cat."

Charles shook his head. "That would've been a good guess, except Mr. Sarnaw died in July. Don't worry, his neighbor took the cat to a friendly shelter where it was adopted. Don't know if the leash was part of the deal."

"Who are you talking about with a cat?"

"I'll give you one more guess. Here's another clue. Who do you know who has a pet snake?"

"Martha Wright," I said, feeling stupid not thinking of her first.

Charles and I met Martha a year ago when Dude Sloan's love of his life Pluto disappeared. After an island-wide search by numerous people, we discovered Martha had taken him in to join her menagerie which included some dozen animals. Martha gladly returned Pluto, apologized for inadvertently thinking he was a stray, and left a lasting impression on me, primarily because of her pet boa constrictor.

"Good guess."

"What about her?"

"She's got cats, Ty has a cat. Martha has a big house, Ty's living in a tiny-tiny four-wheel apartment. Now, the brilliant part. Martha takes in strays. Ty's a stray. Brilliant, right?"

"You think Martha will let Ty move in with her because she takes in strays?"

"How could she not?"

Truth be told, it wasn't a horrible idea. Far from brilliant, but not horrible.

"Why would she?"

"She's an eighty-year-old widow; her poor hubby bit the dust four years ago; she's living in that big house by herself. That lady needs a man around. Ty's almost a man, will do in a pinch. All you have to do is ask her."

"Me?"

"Don't worry, I'll go with you."

Before I could list thirty reasons it'd be a bad idea, the phone rang.

"Okay, troublemaker, what'd you want?" said the less-than-gleeful Cindy LaMond.

"I was talking with Barb at supper about the fire."

Cindy interrupted, "Cheery dinner talk. You sure know how to warm a woman's heart. Get it, fire, warm?"

"Yes, Cindy. Barb was talking about an arson suspect she'd defended. She said there were certain characteristics of most arsonists but was mainly talking about serial arsonists. Her client allegedly set fire to an office building he owned for the insurance."

She interrupted again, "Think you can get to the reason for pestering me before I retire?"

Charles waved for me to put the phone on speaker. Instead of having to repeat everything the Chief said, I hit the speaker icon.

"If the person who set the fire did it because he simply liked to start fires, it may not have anything to do with the residents or the building's owner."

Charles couldn't stand being left out of the conversation. "That makes sense, doesn't it, Chief?"

I heard an audible sigh on the other end of the line.

"Chris, did you get a damned talking parrot, or was that your half-wit friend?"

"Cindy, you know the answer."

"That's what I was afraid of. Did I miss the point of your call somewhere in all that?"

"It's a simple question. Have there been other suspicious fires in the Charleston area?"

"I'm sure there were some in the 1800s. Suppose they were caused by the Yanks, or was it Rebels? Civil War history gets me confused. Charles, you were around then, which was it?"

I smiled and turned to Charles, who said, "Chief, I think Chris means something more recent."

She said, "No."

"No what?" Charles said.

She sighed again. "Did you forget the question? No suspicious fires in the last year or so."

I said, "You sure?"

"Yes, that's what the arson investigator told me when I asked the same question the day he told me it was arson. That means you can throw out the profile for the typical serial arsonist. You know, the profile you and that lovely lady discussed. The same lady who, for reasons beyond anything I can understand, enjoys spending time with you."

I was thinking of a humorous retort, although it would've been wasted. She'd hung up.

Chapter Twenty

Martha's house was four long blocks from the Tides, so I suggested we drive. Charles said it was a great idea, which, I suppose, wasn't as good as his "brilliant" idea that Martha would take Ty, the stray. Her house was a large, two-story, relatively new structure that backed up to the ocean. Martha met us with a look she probably would've given a Mormon missionary. She was no more than five-foot-two, slightly overweight, with dark black hair pulled in a bun. She opened the door a crack.

"Young men, I don't want any."

It was hard to understand what she'd said for the barking dogs nudging the door.

Charles, who didn't accept the concept of rejection, stepped forward, tipped his Tilley, then said, "Martha, I'm Charles Fowler. We met last year when we came looking for Pluto, Dude Sloan's dog. We've also talked in church a time or two."

I hadn't remembered, but Martha was a member of First Light where Charles was a regular.

Martha leaned on her cane, smiled, then said, "Oh, I remember. Sorry, I thought you were some of those church kids going door-to-door, or worse, traveling salesmen. Give me a second to put my killer dogs in another room." She chuckled as she said it. It was at least two minutes before the door opened all the way. "Come in."

"Martha," Charles said as we followed her in the door. "You remember my friend, Chris Landrum, don't you?"

"Sure," she said, in a tone that failed to sound sincere. "Shall we retire to the sitting room?"

The room looked the same as it had a year ago, resembling an animal playhouse more than a sitting room. A three-foot-high, triple deck, carpeted cat tower occupied one corner. On a small table beside the cat tower, there was an oak cabinet like one I remembered from my childhood that contained a record player, or turntable, as they're called today. Assorted animal toys were scattered around. My eyes immediately went to the large aquarium beside one of the three wingback chairs. I was relieved to see the aquarium occupied, relieved because it held a boa constrictor that had to be a mile long. Okay, that's an exaggeration. On a previous visit, Martha shared she often let Squeezy—no, I'm not making that up—roam around the room. She'd said roam, I translated it to mean slither. I took the chair farthest from the aquarium.

Martha had already taken the second farthest chair from Squeezy, so Charles slowly lowered himself in the dog and cat hair infested remaining seat.

"Charles, want to hold Squeezy?"

"Perhaps another time, Martha. Speaking of pets, how many do you have now?"

Instead of answering, she popped up from the chair. "Fellas, want a hot toddy?"

One of the things I'd remembered about our visits last year, was her fondness for the drink, regardless of the time of day.

"No thank you, Martha," Charles said, and repeated, "Perhaps another time."

She lifted the top of the oak cabinet, fiddled with the record player, then said, "Then you can't say no to music of the season."

Neither Charles nor I had time to say, "Perhaps another time," before Alvin and the Chipmunks began their version of "Here Comes Santa Claus." I prayed the volume control wasn't broken since between the scratches on the record and the less-than-appealing voices of the three animated anthropomorphic chipmunks, a Boeing 757's engine would've been quieter.

Martha screamed, "My animals love the Chipmunks. I've got both of their Christmas albums."

Or, I thought that's what she said. The last part was drowned out by Alvin.

"Martha," I yelled, "don't you think it's a little loud?"

She tilted her head my direction, cupped her hand behind her ear, then reached in the cabinet. The volume lowered to bar-conversation levels.

"Sorry, want to repeat that, Chris? Couldn't hear you."

Now that my ears stopped ringing, I didn't feel the need to repeat what I'd said. Instead, I repeated Charles's question. "How many pets do you have?"

She returned to her chair, rubbed her chin, before

saying, "Let's see. It's hard to keep up, you know." She looked toward the door where she'd herded her dogs when we arrived. "Four dogs: Pooch, Lady, Bowser, Ink Spot. No, it's five. I keep forgetting Little Dog. Still have three cats. I'm sure of that. There's Cat One, Cat Two, and Crazy." She shook her head. "Then, got to count Paul."

Charles said, "Your parrot?"

She nodded. "Still got to keep him upstairs, you know. His language would make a sailor blush. Danged hard to teach an old parrot new tricks, or words."

"Know what you mean," Charles said as he glanced my way.

I didn't know, didn't want to know if he wanted rein-forcement, or was calling me old. "Martha," I said, "you still have Davy Crockett?"

She lowered her head, glanced around the room like someone was hiding behind one of the chairs, then said, "You know it's illegal to have a pet raccoon?"

I didn't know for certain, but she'd told us that before. I nodded.

"So, I can't count Davy," she said, winked, then whis-pered, "He's still around."

I nodded a second time.

Charles looked at the aquarium. "Don't forget Squeezy."

"Never, Charles, never." She smiled. "Sure you don't want to hold him?"

"Not this time, Martha."

Alvin and the Chipmunks were now butchering "Silver Bells." Time to move along.

"Martha, we stopped by to—"

She sat up straight in her chair. "I didn't do it."

"Do what?" I asked, figuring it was a reasonable question.

"Whatever you're here to accuse me of, young man."

"Martha, we're not here to accuse you of anything other than being a wonderful lady with some great pets," said Charles the suck-up.

"Oh. The last time you showed up at my door uninvited you accused me of dognapping, stealing that weird hippie's adorable Australian Terrier. Figured you had me on your suspect list if anything bad happens to critters."

"Now Martha," I said, "we know you were doing the right thing with Pluto. He didn't have a collar, he was hungry, you took him in."

"A good deed," Charles added. "Taking in strays is admirable. I've told everyone I know how kind you were to little Pluto."

Told you he was a suck-up. Before Charles pulled out a violin, started singing more praise for Martha, in stark contrast to Alvin trying to sing "Jingle Bells," I'd better refocus the conversation.

"Martha, did you hear about the big, apartment building fire?"

"Lordy, Chris, how could I miss it? It was a block over. Smoke everywhere, sirens blaring. Made my dogs howl nearly as good as Alvin's singing."

"Do you know Ty Striker?"

"Can't say I do."

"He's in his early twenties, thin with long black hair, wears it a ponytail. Works at Bert's."

"Doesn't ring a bell. What about him? Isn't missing, is he?"

Charles piped up, "Not missing, but he's missing a place

to live. He was one of the residents of the building that ain't there no more."

The record player groaned, then clanked, dropping another record on the turntable. Different record, same "performers." The Chipmunks started singing "Jingle Bell Rock."

A high-pitched howl came from the other room.

Martha smiled and nodded toward the room holding her dogs. "Bowser loves this song." She turned to Charles. "Where were we?"

"We were telling you about Ty. He has an adorable kitten, it's got six toes on one of its front paws."

Martha beamed. "A Polydactyl. Just like Hemingway's in Key West."

Charles nodded and I wondered if I was the only person in the country who didn't know about the six-pawed felines.

"Exactly," Charles said.

"What's its name?"

"Lost."

"Oh my, Ty's kitten's lost like that weird hippie's pup."

"No, Martha, Ty's cat is named Lost."

"Oh my, that's a ridiculous name for a cat."

That coming from someone who has cats named Cat One, Cat Two, and a dog named Little Dog.

"It's unusual," I said. "Charles, you want to tell Martha what you were thinking about Ty?"

"That's okay, Chris. You go ahead."

Thanks, coward.

"Martha, we were thinking." I generously didn't say Charles was thinking. "You love animals and have this wonderful large house. It had to be hard to lose your husband a few years back. I bet occasionally things need repairing or there are other things that could use a man's touch."

"You can say that again."

This was going better than expected, I thought.

"We were thinking you could let Ty move in one of your spare rooms until he finds somewhere permanently. He's sleeping in his tiny car."

Her hand flew to her mouth. It may've been my imagination, but her face seemed to turn white, snow-white in the vernacular of the season.

"Heavens to Betsy, no way, young man." Her hand left her face and gripped the arm of her chair. "What would Tommy and Dixie think? Me shacking up with a man. Lordy, no."

Tommy was her late husband, Dixie was her friend who lived across the street.

Alvin was singing "Have Yourself a Merry Little Christmas," but it was doing nothing to make my season bright, my heart feel light, or my troubles out of sight.

Charles appeared to wait for me to continue my sales pitch. I didn't.

"Martha," he said, "I'm certain Dixie would understand. She knows how you like to take in strays. You could consider Ty another stray."

"Young man, I've had a wonderful, long life. I'm not going out of it being accused of being a cougar."

From my limited understanding, Martha would be thirty years or so outside the range of cougars, women seeking younger men.

"Martha, I understand." I didn't. "Charles and I wanted to ask because we knew how kind and caring you were. We don't want to take more of your valuable time."

I stood to leave, when she said, "Now if that Ty fellow wants to bring Lost—I still can't believe he named a cat that—by to visit, that'd be fine. Cat One, Cat Two, and Crazy might like a visitor every now and then."

I said I'd share that information with Ty.

Alvin had stopped singing, Bowser had stopped barking harmony, and I felt anything but in the Christmas spirit as we left Martha leaning on her cane waving bye.

Chapter Twenty-One

"I need a hot toddy after that," Charles said as we got in the car.

"How about a beer at Cal's?"

"A close second."

It was early afternoon when we entered Cal's. The tables were vacant, but three men were seated at the bar drinking lunch. Loretta Lynn was singing "Silver Bells" from the jukebox that would've given Martha's record player a run for being the oldest music machine on the island. Cal was delivering a beer to one of the men. He saw us enter, nodded, then pointed around the room, his way of saying sit anywhere.

We chose a table close to the bar so Cal wouldn't have to go far to serve us. He seldom complained, but his knees were on their last legs, pun intended. Instead of asking what we wanted, he arrived at the table with a Budweiser for Charles, a glass of Cabernet for me.

"Hey, Cal," Charles said, "got anything by Alvin and the Chipmunks on the jukebox?"

Cal plopped down in a chair then squinted at Charles. "Pard, you lost your mind?"

"Don't think so, why?"

"Christmas is my favorite time of year. It's plum near here. This room's decorated, all cheery, festive, ready for that wonderful holiday. Then you come in and suck all the cheer out of me."

"Cal," I said, "what're you talking about?"

Cal looked at the bar to see if any customers needed anything, then back to us. "Back in the day when I was a fledgling country star, eighteen years old, with my first hit 'End of the Story,' I was traveling all over the South singing anywhere that'd have me." He looked at the ceiling. "Ah, those were the days. Anyway, was 1962, lord, I played a lot of bars. Not paying gigs, but tips weren't bad. They also let me sell my records. Most had jukeboxes like mine." He pointed to his ears. "Know what I had to subject these here listening devices to?"

It was beginning to make sense. "Alvin and the Chipmunks?"

"Those damned, fake, striped rodents, singing 'The Alvin Twist.' That horrible song, if you can call it a song, came out the same year my hit flew up the charts." He shook his head. "Can still hear '*If you wanna be smart, if you wanna be wise, take up your fun and exercise. Everybody, do the Alvin Twist.*' Know why I can still hear it?"

Charles, of course, had to know. "Why?"

"Because those damned rodents were singing it on every jukebox in every bar I went in. Over and over, over and over. It got worse after that. Those freakin' rodents came out with their first Christmas album the same year. Talk about kicking Christmas in the head. Why in holy vinyl are you asking about those damned rodents?"

Charles smiled. "So, you don't have any of their Christmas songs on the jukebox?"

Elvis, not Alvin, began singing "Blue Christmas," and I was beginning to think we would have a blue one with Cal and his memories.

"It's not important, Cal," I said. "We wanted to stop to see if there's anything we can do to help you get ready for your party?"

Charles looked at me like, "We were?"

"I appreciate it, boys. Think everything's on schedule. My decorations are up. I got some volunteers coming to help with the food and drinks. Don't know how many folks have told me they're going to be here, but it's a bunch. Thanks for offering."

A customer whistled for Cal. The owner said he'd better earn his keep then headed to the bar.

Charles watched him go. "Think I ought to invite Martha to the Christmas party? She could bring her Chipmunks Christmas albums."

That didn't deserve an answer. I took a sip of wine before saying, "Think we need to talk about who might've set the fire."

"Whoa," Charles said, "you an alien that's done invaded Chris's body? I'm the guy who always wants to butt in police business. Chris always tells me it's none of my concern, that I need to leave it to the cops. What'd you do with my friend?"

"You're right. I know—"

"Of course, I'm right. Umm, remind me why?"

"Charles, I know each of the building's residents. Don't know them well, but it seems that I, we, might know more about them than the police know. It's worth discussing."

"Talk on," he said then took a long draw on his beer.

"Janice Raque is convinced her husband set the fire."

"Why would he? They're divorced, he's moved on with some floozy in Mt. Pleasant, Janice ain't around to fight with him every time they're in here, or wherever else they're butting heads."

"She thinks it's because her lawyer is on Horace's case to get her more support."

Charles said, "You buy that?"

"No, mainly because like you said, the fire was set during the day when there was little chance anyone would've been in the building, little chance anyone would've been hurt."

"Could've been to send a message. Leave me alone or I'll get you. A blazing building would be a powerful way to deliver a message."

"That's possible, but I'd put him low on my list."

"Okay, moving along, who would've wanted to burn Rose and Luke's apartment out from under them?"

I hadn't shared what Rose told me about her ex being on Folly the day before the fire. I took another sip knowing I'd need it once Charles started haranguing me for not telling him sooner. I took a deep breath then shared what Rose had told me.

Charles had started to take a drink, instead, he set the bottle on the table, more accurately, pounded the bottle on the table. "You didn't think that was important enough ... never mind. Rose's hubby sounds too stupid to be a bank vice president if he thought she'd come crawling back to him if her apartment went up in smoke."

"I agree. I mentioned him because we know he was here the day before the fire. Don't you think that's a big coincidence?"

"Do we know if he was here the day of the fire?"

"No."

Charles pointed in the direction of the ocean. "I'll nose around the Tides. My innocent-looking face makes people tell me stuff they shouldn't."

His countless questions didn't hurt him getting information either. "Good idea, although there are many other places he could've stayed."

"Nick Matthews," Charles said.

"Aimee's fiancée?"

"He could've done it. Didn't Ty tell us he mumbled something like you'll get yours?"

"Yes."

"There you go. Suspect number one."

"How're we going to find out more about him?" I said out loud, although talking more to myself.

Charles picked my phone off the table, pointed it at me. "Call Cindy. Maybe Nick has a record or is known by the local cops for burning buildings."

"I'll call her later."

"Don't worry, I won't let you forget."

Cal returned to the table. "Get you boys anything else to drink?"

Charles looked at his bottle. "Not yet. What if we want something to eat?"

"I'll point you to some good restaurants," Cal said, then

pushed his Stetson back on his head. "Neil ain't here, and I'm not in the mood for fixin' food."

"Speaking of Neil," Charles said, "know if he pissed off anyone enough to torch his building?"

"Don't know about him, but if it had a trio of damned chipmunks living there, I would've torched it myself."

Fifty years later, Alvin and his compatriots were still under Cal's skin.

"What about Neil?" I said to bring him back to the twenty-first century.

"I asked him. He said it could've been his old boss. Seems Neil turned the cheatin', thievin' crook's name over to the IRS. The feds came down on him like a pile of manure."

Neil had told Charles and me the same thing.

"That'd be a strong motive," Charles said.

I said, "He also mentioned something about a man he threw out of the bar."

"Don't remember that," Cal said.

"No," Charles said, "the bar in Charleston where he's a bouncer."

Cal said, "I'd stick with the IRS busted boss. Guys get thrown out of bars all the time. They bitch and groan, threaten everyone around, then sober up, before starting all over again. No biggie."

"You're probably right," I said. "Has Neil found a place to live?"

"Far as I know, he's still at the Holliday Inn. Says it costs him nearly everything he makes."

"It'd be nice, Christmaslike, if someone would take him in until he finds a cheaper place, wouldn't it?" Charles said, glancing at me out the corner of his eye.

One of the men at the bar called for another beer. Cal left to meet the need, and Hank Locklin broke the string of Christmas songs from the jukebox with "Please Help Me, I'm Falling."

"That brings us to Noelle," I said to move away from Neil's housing plight. "Let me tell you what she said yesterday."

"Is it like what you learned from Janice and didn't think it was important enough to tell me?"

"Charles, give me a chance, I'll tell you."

Charles held up his empty beer bottle. "Yo, Cal, I need another one of those. Chris is driving me to drink."

I told him about my encounter with Noelle after I saw her casing the Post Office. He was relatively calm until I got to the part about the note on her truck.

"You thought that clue wasn't important enough to lead this discussion with?"

Cal set a second Budweiser on the table then asked if I needed another glass of wine. I declined. Charles said he may need it before I drove him crazy.

Cal added, "Crazier," then headed to the bar.

"I don't know what we can do with that information," I said.

"You can add it to the list of things to talk to Cindy about."

"I'll do that. Let me tell you what Barb said about arsonists."

"Is it something else you should've told me before today?"

"No," I said, more defensively than I had intended. "Learned it last night."

I proceeded to tell him about Barb's research about

arsonists, how it appeared whoever burned the apartment building probably wouldn't be considered a serial arsonist, but someone who burned it for a specific purpose. The most likely suspect would be the building's owner Russell O'Leary."

"Insurance?"

"Probably."

"He has money trouble?" Charles asked.

"Three months behind on the mortgage."

"Does Cindy know?"

"That's who told me. She's already looking into it. He also told her he was at a meeting in Atlanta, but the story was weak. He didn't remember where he stayed, paid cash, lots of wiggle room in his alibi."

Charles took a sip of the second beer, started peeling the label off the bottle, then said, "What do we do now?"

"Enjoy looking at Cal's Christmas decorations, his beautiful trees, then think how lucky we are to have a place to live."

Merle Haggard sang "If We Make It Through December."

Chapter Twenty-Two

I called Cindy after Charles and I had gone our separate ways.

"What now?" she said then sighed.

As strange as it seems, I was happier to hear that rude response than her trying to be friendly. Cindy was being Cindy.

"Have you talked to Noelle Ward about the fire?"

"You mean Imani Marshall?"

"Yes."

"She want to confess starting it?"

"Don't believe so, but if you say pretty please, she'll tell you about a note slipped under her windshield wiper a week before the fire."

"Did the person who wrote it say he or she was going to incinerate the building, then sign the note?"

"Noelle didn't mention it. It told her to get off the island or something like that."

"Was your new buddy Noelle ever going to share this with the police?"

"I asked. She said it wouldn't do any good." I didn't tell Cindy that Noelle wasn't going to law enforcement because her novel's protagonist wouldn't.

"I'd like her to tell me that. Do you know where she's staying?"

"In her truck. I bet your crack police force could find one big Dodge Ram pickup without much trouble."

"You have more faith in them then I have. Would you happen to have Ms. Ward/Marshall's phone number?"

I not only told her I did but gave it to her.

"Cindy, now that you're on the phone, I have another question."

"Of course, you do, Charles in waiting."

"Do you know Nick Matthews?"

"No. Who's he?"

"How about Aimee Mason?"

"Chris, there are two thousand residents on Folly Beach. Are you planning on asking about each of them until I admit knowing someone?"

I chuckled. "No."

"So, who are Nick and Aimee?"

I shared what little I knew about them, omitting any mention of Lost, Ty's cat.

"Let me see if I have this straight. Ty was hitting on Aimee who happens to be Nick's fiancée. Nick didn't take kindly to it and maybe-kind-of-sort-of threatened Ty. How am I doing?"

"Perfect. No wonder you're Chief."

"Your theory is Nick thought Ty failed to grasp the importance of his maybe-kind-of-sort-of threat and burned an entire apartment building to communicate more strongly his objection to Ty's advances on his gal?"

"You've got it."

"That sounds like a stretch."

"Yes, but—"

Cindy interrupted, "Hold the but, the one with one T. Because you're such a friend, a pain in the butt with two Ts friend, I'll see if I can find Nick and have a pleasant talk. You don't happen to have his number, do you?"

"Sorry, no. By the way, how are Rose and Luke doing?"

"Luke's pestering Larry for a raise. Says he wants the extra money to buy his mom a nice Christmas present. Rose is trying to use some of her highfalutin education on me. Can you imagine her learnin' me proper grammar? I told her I'm dumber than a pretzel compared to her college students. I think she's figurin' that out."

Cindy is one of the smartest people I know. Her grammar may not always live up to textbook standards, but she's an effective communicator. She's also one of the most stubborn people I've run across. Rose will have her hands full. I wanted to ask if Rose told her about her ex's visit the day before the fire, but honored Rose's request that I not share it.

"Has she said much about the fire?"

"More about how rough it's been losing everything except the clothes on her back. She knows how lucky she and Luke were. The arson investigator figured the fire started in the apartment next to theirs, so they would've been close to the origination point if they'd been home."

"Does she think it had anything to do with them?"

"Why would it? She just moved here. They didn't know anybody, didn't even know others who lived in the building."

Which means Rose hadn't said anything about her ex's visit.

"Just curious."

Cindy laughed. "More than anything, Rose and Luke are putting their energy into decorating the house. Larry and I've never done anything more than put a wreath on the front door. No tree, no wrapped presents, no stockings hung by the chimney with care. Crap, we don't even have a chimney. By the time Christmas rolls around, Larry is shuffling around like an elf zombie. Tell him I said that, and you'll be hung by a rope by somebody's chimney."

I chuckled. "Your term of endearment is safe."

"Rose said our house shouldn't be decorated for Christmas the same way it is for Groundhog Day. She found an artificial tree in the attic, must've come with the place. They cleared a century of dust off it, plopped it down in the family room. Then Luke convinced Larry to give him strands of lights from the store so he and his mom could string them around the tree. Then Santa's little helpers went to Harris Teeter, bought wrapping paper, and candy canes. Now they're hanging on nearly everything you can hook a cane on."

"That's great, Cindy."

"I'll admit, it looks good. I put my foot down when she suggested I bake Christmas cookies. Luke said not to worry, he and his mom will bake them. I hope Larry will have enough energy left in his petite body to enjoy everything. Hell, I may even buy him a Christmas present. What man doesn't want a snow globe?"

"That's what we live for, Cindy."

"Perfect. I'll be sure to tell Larry you said that."

I hoped she was kidding. "Ho, Ho, Ho! Anything I can do to help?"

"Come to the house after Christmas to take down all the stuff Rose and Luke used to transform our humble abode into a Christmas village."

"Anything else?"

"Yeah, I'd love to spend more time talking about Christmas but I have to see if I can find Noelle, or whatever her name is, living in a pickup truck; Nick, the jealous fiancée; plus any other person who may've been on Folly in the last week who might've started the fire."

"That should keep you busy for a few minutes."

"I wish."

"One more thing before you go to solve the mystery. Don't forget Cal's annual Christmas bash."

"Gee, Chris, how could I forget, he only does it every Christmas. I'm not old like you. I don't have to be reminded to get up every morning."

"I was thinking you and Larry might want to bring Rose and Luke by to meet some others on Folly."

"Good thought. I'll talk to them about it. Larry, of course, will sleep all day after he drags his tiny butt in from working ninety-four hours a day at the store."

"In addition to Rose teaching you proper grammar, you may see if she can refresh your knowledge of math."

I'm certain she was going to thank me for the suggestion, but the phone went dead before she had a chance.

Chapter Twenty-Three

The most likely person with a reason to burn the apartment building was its owner, Russell O'Leary. He was three months behind on his mortgage, one of the apartment units had been vacant for several months which would've made it more difficult to cover the mortgage. He claimed to have been in Atlanta at a meeting on the day of the fire but told Cindy he didn't stay at the hotel where the event was held. He said he'd rented a room at a nearby hotel whose name he couldn't remember. A feeble alibi at best. So, how do I prove it?

I didn't know Russell but knew someone who might. Bob Howard, a friend, and former Realtor who'd handled countless sales in the Charleston area.

"Good afternoon, Bob," I said after he answered on the third ring.

"Well if it isn't my worthless acquaintance who thinks he's too good to spend time with his good buddy."

Despite having had a successful career in real estate, Bob

had the personality of a hippopotamus and nearly the same weight, yet, for reason's unknown, we'd become friends after he helped me find my cottage on Folly, the space I'd rented for Landrum Gallery, plus sharing information over the years allowing me to catch a couple of bad guys.

I ignored his comment, a wise decision when spending time around Bob. "Do you know Russell O'Leary?"

"Yes."

I waited for more. It was a waste of time.

"What do you know about him?"

"Chris, I figure the CIA, KGB, NCAA, or one of those other evil agencies has this phone bugged. Suppose you'll need to come over to hear it in person. Oh yeah, while you're here, you can buy a cheeseburger, double order of fries to share with me, plus some of that nasty red wine you sip in the winter."

"Will you be there in an hour?"

"Hell yes, damned slave-driver Al won't let me leave."

I hung up on him. It felt good.

When Bob retired from selling real estate, he bought Al's Bar near downtown Charleston. While it's too long a story to relay here, suffice to say Bob knew as much about running a bar as a jumbo shrimp knows about needlepoint. He bought it because his long-time friend Al Washington, the previous owner, was suffering serious health issues after running the bar for decades while raising nine adopted kids, much of that time as a single dad. Bob couldn't stand seeing Al suffer.

Forty-five minutes later, I was pulling in a rare empty parking space a half-block from Al's in an area of town near two hospital complexes. Other than the often-expanding health care facilities, much of the residential area would be considered pre-gentrification. If you'd called Al's Bar a hole in the wall, you'd be giving it too much credit. It was in a concrete-block building it shared with a Laundromat. The building hadn't been clothed in fresh paint since the Vietnam War. Regardless of its physical condition, I was certain Al's cheeseburgers were the best in the state. Bob claimed they were the best in the country. He could be right.

I stepped from late-afternoon daylight into cave-like darkness to be greeted by Al, who since Bob purchased the bar, served as the business's Walmart greeter.

"Praise the Lord, you're here," he said, gave me a warm, extended hug, then whispered, "Blubber Bob's been asking every two minutes if you were here yet."

The only illumination in the room came from a Budweiser and Budweiser Light neon signs behind the aging bar, but Bob was seated close enough to see each time the door opened. In other words, he had no reason to pester Al about my arrival.

Al was eighty-two-years-old, with short, gray hair, coffee-stained teeth, with skin the color somewhere between dark brown and light black. He looked as well-worn as the room's yard-sale tables and chairs.

"Old man," came a bellowing voice from the rear of the room, "stop hugging on the damned scrawny honkie so he can get over here and spend money. How in the hell am I going to pay your astronomical salary if you don't let customers blow their cash in here?"

That was Bob at his best. Al had the good sense not to remind Bob he was working free. Two men were seated at a table near the large plate-glass window, the lower-half painted black to provide privacy for the diners. They were sipping beer and playing cards. A pile of wooden matches was in front of each of them which I suspected had value other than for starting fires.

Other than the cardplayers, the bar was empty except for Al, Bob, and me. Al said he'd throw my cheeseburger on the grill if I promised to keep Bob quiet. I told him I'd do my best. During busy times, which were fewer and fewer, a part-time cook fixed the food. I hated that Al had to move around that much but knew that the chance of Bob manning the grill was about the same as him being named Pope.

"About time you got here," Bob said as I squeezed in my side of the booth, a space barely wide enough for me since Bob had taken up twice the normal space on the other side of the table. "Nosing in police business again?"

"Why do you say that?"

"Oh, could be because you called to ask if I knew Russell O'Leary who happens to own the building someone turned black and flat a couple of blocks from your house. Or, could be because you stick your pasty white nose in everything bad happening on Folly. How am I doing?"

Before I could answer, one of the cardplayers raised his hand and hollered to Al, "How about a couple more beers?"

Bob, being the customer-friendly, service-oriented bar owner, said, "Marvin, can't your Afro eyes see the man's busy fixing food for my young friend here?"

Bob was white; ninety-five percent of his customers African American. After Bob bought the bar, Al told me the main reason he wanted to stay on was to prevent a race riot in the place where he'd spent most of his work life. The more the regulars learned that Bob didn't like black people, they realized he didn't like brown, yellow, white, or any other color people. He was a textbook example of an equal-opportunity offender. He didn't like anyone, or so it appeared.

Marvin mumbled something under his breath, then went to the cooler and got the drinks. Bob mumbled something that sounded like, "Thanks, Marvin," but I had a hard time believing he could've said the word thanks.

Marvin returned to the card game, riot averted, for now. Bob turned back to me.

"Where was I," he said. "Oh yeah, you were going to tell me I was right about you nosing in police business."

I agreed but wasn't about to give him the satisfaction of hearing it.

"What do you know about O'Leary?"

"He's a heavy-truck mechanic at a shop over here. Decent income, but hard work, long hours. When his dad died a few years back, he inherited the building where you're snooping where you shouldn't."

Al made his way to the table, set a cheeseburger with a double order of fries in front of me. Before I'd arrived, Bob told him what I'd want, and what he'd want with the extra order of fries. Al also set a glass of wine beside my plate.

"Set your bony ass down while I tell my good-buddy Chris how brilliant I am."

Al lowered himself beside me. "Don't need to hear it. You say it every day."

"Old man, the truth will set you free."

Al rolled his eyes, as the sounds of the Four Tops' hit "Reach Out, I'll Be There," reverberated off the walls.

Bob yelled, "Marvin, you do that?"

Marvin smiled. "Yes, Master Bob. You needed some good music."

"Next time you punch those numbers in the jukebox I'm

getting a restraining order to keep you from entering this fine dining, drinking establishment ever again."

Marvin's smile turned to a laugh. "Yes, Master Bob."

Bob turned back to Al and me. "Damned radicals."

"Bob, how do you know so much about O'Leary?"

"He walked into my office soon after inheriting the building. Said he knew everything there was to know about fixing a Peterbilt but nothing about owning an apartment building. Wanted to talk about selling. I worked up comps and met to talk to him about the details of selling a multi-unit structure. He pondered it for a couple of weeks before calling to say he and his wife talked it over. They have two teenagers, college-age by now, I guess. Much to my thinning wallet's dismay, they decided to hold on to the building. Said they wanted it to be a legacy they could leave to their kids, which meant no money for me to leave to my kids."

"Bob," Al said, "you ain't got no kids."

"Hell, Al, get with the program. I was being figurative-speaking-like, making the point that his gain was my loss."

"Sounded stupid-like to me," Al said.

I agreed with Al. "Bob, is that all you know about O'Leary?"

"That's more than you knew when you walked in."

"True. So, that's all?"

"Nope."

"Heavens, Bob. Tell the man what you know. Use plain English while you're doing it."

"Hush, old man. Let me tell the story the way I want."

Instead of smacking the fry out of Bob's mouth, Al smiled, then leaned back in the chair.

Despite tremendous differences ranging from skin color to socioeconomic background, to kindness to others, Bob and Al had been friends for decades; they'd do anything for each other.

"After you called to tell me you'd love to come over and buy a cheeseburger, I called a realtor I know over your way to see if he knew anything about Russell. He said rumors were flying that the mechanic turned landlord was in deep financial straits. Late paying bills, months behind on his mortgage, one kid in college, one in trouble with the law."

"Is that all?"

"What more do you want, his social security number and cholesterol level? I suppose you think he torched the building for the insurance."

"Maybe."

Bob stuffed another fry in his mouth, then said, "Hell, I know I would've."

Chapter Twenty-Four

Another below-average temperature the week before Christmas greeted me as I stepped outside for the walk next door for coffee, something to eat, and with luck, a chance to check on Ty. Three construction workers were standing around the large coffee urn—one pouring coffee, two adding sugar and milk to their caffeinated drink. I drew a cup after the workers headed to the exit, then moved to the cabinet holding three large Cinnamon rolls, where Preacher Burl Costello was holding two boxes of prepackaged donuts.

"Morning Burl, didn't your chef show up to fix breakfast?"

As he smiled, his milk-chocolate colored mustache wiggled like a caterpillar inching its way along his upper lip. "And a good morning to you as well, Brother Chris. One of my fantasy dreams is for a chef to take up residence at Hope House. Until then, the bakery in, umm," he looked at the bottom of the donut package. "Cleveland, Ohio, will have to prepare our morning meals. My skills are limited to burning toast and offering a prayer."

I pointed to the shelf where I was eying my breakfast. "Burning toast would be an upgrade in my culinary skills. Don't suppose you have vacancies since we talked the other day?"

Burl's smile transitioned to a frown plus a slow head shake. "Still full. Are some of the residents of the burned building still without somewhere to hang their hats?"

I glanced around looking for Ty, not seeing him, I said, "Unfortunately yes. Rose Wheeler and her son are the only ones who've found accommodations."

"Are they the relatives of our outstanding Chief?"

"She's Cindy's sister, Luke, Cindy's nephew. The others are living in their vehicles or staying at the Holliday Inn."

"Brother Chris, I have faith our community will come together to aid the displaced."

"I wish I had that much faith."

He smiled and patted my arm. "Tis the season of faith, Brother Chris. The season of faith."

As if on cue, Ty appeared at my side. He asked if he could help us find something. He had on what looked like the same shirt he'd been wearing the last time I'd seen him. His ponytail shined like it was covered with a layer of oil.

I introduced Ty to Preacher Burl.

"Preacher, Ty is one of the displaced residents I was talking about."

Burl set the donuts on the table, then put one arm around Ty. "Brother Ty, I'm terribly sorry about your loss of residence."

Ty took a step back from Burl. "No biggie, Preacher. I've lived in worse places than in my car. Besides, Lost is safe."

Burl looked at the young man like he'd look at three-legged deer. "Brother Ty, don't believe I understand."

I wouldn't have either if I hadn't known about Lost. "Preacher Burl, Ty is living in his Miata. Lost is the name of his adorable kitten that was in his car during the fire."

"Oh," Burl said, still looking confused. "It's nice meeting you, Brother Ty. I have faith you'll find somewhere to live, perhaps with more living space than your car. Gentlemen, I hate to run but need to get back to the house with breakfast or I'll have several residents ready to move me to my vehicle."

"Preacher," I said, "will you be at Cal's Christmas party?"

"I wouldn't miss Brother Cal's event, although I'd be more inclined to be there if that old country singer didn't feel the need to drag me on stage to join him in a Christmas song."

The last two Christmas parties, Cal thought singing a duet with Burl was something the group would enjoy. The bar's owner said it combined the spirit of the holiday with the religious significance of the sacred event. Burl thought there must be better ways to communicate the message, but went along with Cal.

"Preacher, that's the highlight of the event."

"Not to me, Brother Chris. Not to me,"

Burl headed to the register.

Ty watched him go, then said, "He talks funny, doesn't he? Several customers told me they go to his church. I should give it a try. He has more faith than I have about me finding somewhere to live."

I shared more information about First Light, Hope

House, then added, "Ty, another reason I came in was to see how you're doing."

"That's kind of you, Mr. Landrum. I'm doing peachy." He snapped his fingers. "There was one thing I wanted to mention when I saw you." He stared at me like he wanted me to say something.

"Now would be a good time."

He nodded. "Remember I told you about Aimee's fiancée?"

"Nick something."

"Nick Matthews. He came in yesterday. I didn't see him at first. He was over by the beer cooler. I was stocking the book rack, know where I mean?"

"Yes."

"He got a six-pack, then walked close to me. He had this big look on his face. Looked like one of those Cheshire cat grins."

"Did he say anything?"

"Not a word, but figured the look was like him telling me he burnt the building, a smirk because he did it."

"Ty, you're certain he didn't say anything?"

"Certain."

I wasn't aware of laws against smirking but thought he should tell the police his suspicions.

"Ty, I doubt it'll do any good but I suggest you tell Chief Lamond the next time she's in."

"I will if you think it's a good idea but if I was the Chief and some kid told me he was reporting a smirk, I'd nod and forget it."

"Ty, she might do that but she's trying to figure out who set the fire. Anything related, regardless of how small or inconsequential, may help."

"If you say so," he said, sounding as convincing as I had suggesting it. "Better get back to work. Don't know what I'd do if I lost this job." He laughed. "I'd hate to have to give up my luxurious living quarters."

I was impressed by how well he was taking his uncomfortable situation. I couldn't handle it as well.

Chapter Twenty-Five

I called Neil after I got home. He'd told me a lot about
the man he'd sicked the IRS on, but little about the
person who'd threatened him after being bounced
from the Charleston bar.

"Neil, are you at Cal's?"

"I go in at four. Why?"

"I was wondering about something you'd said. Thought
I'd drop in if you were working."

"You can come tonight, or I could meet you somewhere
now. The less time I spend in this room the better."

We agreed to meet at St. James Gate, a restaurant on the
corner of Center Street and Ashley Avenue that prides itself
on being a "proper Irish pub." From its distinct green and
tan exterior to the dark wood and stone interior, the restaurant has the feel of how I pictured an Irish pub.

I would've preferred to sit on the back patio, but the
temperature made that impractical, so I chose a table in

front of the window facing Center Street. A half-dozen customers were at the bar. Four men sat at a table in the center of the room with two of them staring at laptop computers, most likely salespersons discussing whatever salespersons discuss. A server wearing a green and white T-shirt with a three-leaf clover over his heart was quick to the table. If I drank beer, I would've automatically ordered Guinness, the beer of choice in the pub. The server appeared disappointed when I stuck with water. He cheered slightly when I told him I was waiting on someone and might order more when my guest arrives.

I didn't wait long. Neil came in the door and headed my way. The server arrived with my water at the same time. Neil did what was expected in the Irish pub when he ordered Guinness and a menu. The server looked at me with an expression that said, "See, that's what you're supposed to do," then went to get Neil's drink.

"What's on your mind, Chris?"

Nothing like getting to the point, I thought. I told him I was wondering how he was doing, the same thing I'd said to Ty.

"Okay, I guess. Cal has been kind to give me extra hours, so I have enough money to replace some of the stuff lost in the fire. My car's a gas guzzler, so I cut back on my job in Charleston. Walking to Cal's helps save some."

"Still living in the Holliday Inn?"

"Yes, but I'd love to get out of there. They gave me a good rate, but I still can't afford it. Also, I can't stand being pent up in the small room. This time of year, it's even worse. It … never mind."

"Worse because of the holidays?"

"Sort of."

That's the kind of comment Charles would be all over. I liked to think I wasn't quite as pushy.

"Neil, when we were talking the other day, you said one of your customers in Charleston threatened you after you, umm, evicted him."

"Nothing unusual. It happens more than you might think. Alcohol does strange things to folks."

The gods of irony arrived the same time the server arrived with Neil's alcoholic drink. The server asked if we were ready to order. Neil said the beer was all he needed for now, so I ordered a soft drink instead of food. I didn't know if Neil wasn't hungry or didn't have money for lunch.

"Neil, didn't you say the man you threw out threatened you?"

"Yeah." He chuckled. "They all do."

"Could he have started the fire for revenge?"

"I suppose so, but he didn't know where I lived."

"Could he have followed you home?"

Neil smiled. "Not that night. I don't think he was in any condition to find his nose, much less my apartment."

"Seen him since then?"

"Once or twice. He's a regular."

"He give you more trouble?"

"He made a couple of smart-ass comments, nothing more."

"No more threats?"

"Not really. I don't think he started the fire. If anyone did because of me, it was the guy who owns the plant where I worked."

"Do you have a reason to think that anything other than because he'd be angry?"

"He's got a temper. I remember several times where he yelled at an employee, or when he pounded his fist on a wall."

"Have you seen him since you turned him in?"

Neil took a sip of beer, looked out the window, then said, "No."

"He never directly threatened you?"

"No."

Other than two people who may have a beef with him, Neil didn't know anything to tie them to the fire, which brings me back to something he'd said, or more accurately, hadn't said about this time of year being worse than other times.

"Neil, what did you mean when you said this time of year was bad?"

He took another sip as he resumed staring out the window. I was afraid I'd irritated him.

He finally turned to me. "My dad died three days before Christmas. I was seventeen."

"Neil, I'm sorry. What happened?"

"Cancer. He'd been sick for months. We knew his time was short, but he told mom and me he wanted to be here one more Christmas. He didn't make it."

"That would be a good reason to be depressed this time of year. Again, I'm sorry."

He slowly shook his head. "There's more."

The server returned and asked if Neil wanted another beer. He nodded but didn't say anything. I told the server I was fine.

Neil watched him leave, then said, "I was married once."

"Oh," I said.

"She was the most wonderful person I ever knew. Married five years, five wonderful years."

Do I ask what happened? The server was back before I decided.

Neil took a long draw on the beer, then said, "Three years ago, Lisa, that was her name, went to visit her parents. They lived thirty miles from our house. Her car was T-boned by a drunk driver. Killed her instantly."

"Neil, I'm terribly sorry."

"Was Christmas Eve. Know what happened to the damned drunk?"

I shook my head.

"Airbag broke his little finger. Lisa dies and he gets his damned pinkie broke."

Not knowing what to say, I shook my head.

He took a sip, looked out the window, hopped out of the chair, and headed to the restroom. It was becoming clear why this time of the year was rough on Neil. It was also clear I was running out of ways to say sorry.

Neil returned, gave me a feeble smile, then said, "Know what I did the next Christmas?"

I was afraid to guess. "What?"

"Got arrested. Aggravated assault."

"What happened?"

"Sitting in a bar, feeling sorry for myself. Christmas Eve, a year to the day I lost Lisa." He held up his beer. "Drinking way too many of these. A guy sitting next to me started ragging on the gal bartender. Bitching about her being slow. I blew a gasket. Before I knew it, we were exchanging blows, then I was being hauled away by what must've been a dozen cops. Chris, ain't nothing good about spending Christmas in jail."

"Neil, no wonder this is a bad time of year."

"I'd be lying if I said it wasn't." He hesitated, then added, "You're the only person I've told all this to. I'd appreciate it if you didn't share it with anyone."

"It won't leave this table."

He smiled. "Thank you. Know what's picked me up more than anything?"

"What?"

"Cal. Watching that old crooner get so excited about Christmas. Helping him put up the trees, decorating the bar. Being part of something positive about the holiday has kept me from thinking too much about the bad ones. He's a lifesaver."

Before I left St. James Gate, Neil had put most of his negative thoughts behind him. I encouraged him to talk about working at Cal's. He shared a few humorous things he'd witnessed, how interesting it was to spend time with Cal reliving his experiences with many of the country legends from fifty years ago, and a few quirky regulars who frequented the bar. Neil said he wasn't a country music fan, but hanging around Cal, he had a new appreciation for the genre. He especially had a growing appreciation for Cal, his outlook on life, his tolerance of all people. I didn't know how long Neil's good mood would last since we were only a handful of days before Christmas, but when we went our separate ways, he was laughing.

———

I was crossing Center Street when I heard a horn, turned, and saw it was coming from a black Dodge Ram pickup. The truck, driven by Noelle, I assumed, pulled off the road in front of me. I moved to the driver's side and was greeted by a smiling Noelle Ward.

"Good to see you, Chris. Where you headed?"

"Nowhere in particular."

"Want to hop in? I could use some company."

I walked around to the passenger door, opened it, slid in, then looked at the back seat that held a sleeping bag, a small suitcase, and three Walmart bags.

"Still driving your apartment?"

Noelle, dressed in a black sweatshirt, black jeans, and red tennis shoes, laughed, then said, "Got some new duds at Walmart. All I have to do now is figure out how to get cable TV in here."

"Gets a little tight back there, doesn't it?"

She laughed. "One big advantage of being short and scrawny is I fit almost anywhere."

She waved at Ty standing in front of Bert's, drove past my house, then proceeded to her former residence.

She shook her head, then said, "Sad looking mess. It wasn't Shangri-La, but provided decent, almost decent housing."

The rubble looked exactly like it had the day after the fire.

"Sad, especially for those who were displaced."

"I have faith something will work out for all of us. After all, it's Christmas. Time for miracles, they say."

A blue Toyota Prius slowed, started to turn into the lot, then continued out Ashley Avenue.

Noelle watched the car slow and then leave. "That's the landlord."

"Have you talked to him since the fire?"

"No."

"Hear anything else about who started it?"

"Not really, or not really anything credible. I told you before that I'm spending time walking around observing people. Vacationers act different than locals, youngsters act way different than, umm, old-timers."

"Like me?"

She grinned. "No, not you, I mean old people."

"Ever thought about becoming a diplomat?"

"Too much work."

"For me, it'd be easier than writing a book."

"Anyway, in addition to observing folks, I've talked to several, mainly to see how they react to a stranger. A few want to talk about the fire." She chuckled. "It was hard getting some to stop talking about it. Besides the Christmas parade, the fire was the biggest thing that's happened around here in a while."

"It doesn't take much to get folks gossiping."

She stepped out of the truck and leaned against the hood. I joined her in front of the vehicle.

Noelle stared at the ruins then said, "One old man in the Crab Shack said he was certain the fire was started by a pyromaniac traveling from New York to Miami. The old guy said the man stopped here on his way to practice starting fires. He also said President Kennedy is living in a beach house on Kiawah."

"He lost credibility on that one, didn't he?"

"Did with me. Did you hear the fire started in the middle unit, first floor?"

"Yes, it was vacant, I believe."

"Vacant several months. Another guy at the Crab Shack told me he heard the fire was started by a kid sneaking in the empty apartment to smoke. The man couldn't explain how the kid spread gasoline around to make the fire accelerate."

"Noelle, that probably scratches the surface of rumors going around about the fire."

"Chris, there's one other thing. It could be my imagination." She smiled. "Novelists have big imaginations you know. Anyway, a couple of days before the fire, I noticed a guy standing back there." She pointed to the back of the lot. "Seems he was staring at my apartment. The reason he got my attention was that I'd swear I saw him three other times in recent weeks. I noticed because he was always looking around like he thought he was being followed."

"What'd he look like?"

"White dude, little older than me, long shaggy black hair."

"What about clothes?"

"Had them on every time I saw him," she said, then laughed.

"Cute."

"Sorry. He looked like every other dude. Jeans, sweatshirt, backward ball cap, think it was red."

"Anything else?"

"Not really. If I was putting him in my book, he'd be someone on the run, because of the way he kept looking around like he was worried about someone seeing him."

"Seen him since the fire?"

She looked toward the sky, then back at me, "Don't think so. Now you know everything I know about the guy."

"If you would, call me if you see him again. The police chief and I are friends. I can have her check him out."

"Deal. By the way, I was in the bookstore yesterday. The lady who owns it said you two are an item."

"We've been seeing each other a while."

"She's really nice."

I agreed.

Chapter Twenty-Six

I was to meet Barb for supper at Loggerhead's Beach Grill located across the street from her condo in the Charleston Oceanfront Villas. I was there fifteen minutes before the time we were to meet. The restaurant has one of the nicest outdoor decks on the island, but tonight was too cool to enjoy it. As I was walking across the parking lot, I noticed a man getting out of a blue Prius. He was middle-aged, six-foot-tall, average weight with a slight limp. I followed him up the steps and into the building where he took a stool at the bar. Most of the indoor tables were taken, so I was fortunate to get one along the wall. I wasn't certain, but the Prius was the color of the one Noelle said belonged to Russell O'Leary.

I didn't give the man another thought and ordered a Diet Coke while I waited for Barb. She was seldom late, but unlike Charles, she assumed on-time meant on-time, so I wasn't surprised she wasn't here yet. I was beginning to wonder when it was ten minutes after the time she was to arrive. I didn't wonder long. The phone rang with her name on the screen.

"On your way?"

"Not yet. Two groups came in as I was closing. It was as if they just realized Christmas was four days away. They're rummaging through the books trying to do all their Christmas shopping. It'll be a little while before I can get there. Want to postpone, or am I worth waiting for?"

I'm far from the smartest person in my orbit but knew there was only one acceptable answer. "Of course you're worth waiting for. Take your time."

"I appreciate it."

Three couples were at the door waiting for a table. Rather than hogging the real estate for no telling how long, I told the server I'd be at the bar. Besides, it'd give me a chance to introduce myself to the man I suspected to be the apartment building's owner. I took the bar-height seat next to him, then realized I had no logical way of identifying myself or asking about the fire. It didn't help that he was gripping his beer glass with both hands and staring at the liquid it contained like his mind was a thousand miles away.

I did my Charles imitation. "Hi, I'm Chris. You live around here?"

His hands never left the glass, but his head tilted slightly in my direction. "No."

Charles does Charles way better than I do.

"Then you probably didn't hear about the big fire on Folly a week ago."

This time he took one hand off the glass, then turned toward me. "Who'd you say you are again?"

"Chris Landrum."

He reached out in a motion I assumed meant to shake

my hand. I shook his wet hand as he said, "I'm Russell O'Leary. You won't believe this, but it was my building that burned."

"You're kidding, that's terrible. I hear it's a total loss."

He sighed. "Unfortunately."

"What caused it?"

"They said arson."

"I'm sorry, Russell. Who would've done that?"

I thought that was better than asking if he'd torched it.

He shrugged.

"Own it long?"

"Been in the family twenty-three years. Dad had it until he passed a few years ago. I got the building. Inherited it and all its problems."

"Problems?"

He hesitated long enough for me to think my question had gone too far.

Finally, he said, "I'm a mechanic, big trucks. I didn't know anything about maintaining a building like that. Dad got the best years out of it, I got the leaky pipes, busted air-conditioners, wiring problems, outside constantly needing paint, that's not even counting deadbeat tenants who'd rather pay for cigarettes and cell phones than rent."

I remembered what Bob Howard had said about Russell considering selling the building.

"Ever think about selling?"

"Only every day, and twice in the middle of the night when I'd get a call about something wrong. What'd you say your name was again?"

His glass was empty. "Chris. Let me buy you another beer."

He glanced at his watch, then smiled, finally. "I never

turn down a drink."

I waved for the bartender, ordered a beer for Russell, said I was okay with my drink.

"If it was such a headache, how come you didn't sell? From what I hear, the market's strong."

"Don't think I didn't come close a time or two. I've got two kids, guess they're not really kids anymore. They're eighteen and nineteen, almost grown men. Every time I said something about selling, they went bananas. Say they're going to take over, help do all the work, want it for their inheritance. My wife is on their side."

His second beer arrived, and he didn't waste time taking a long pull.

"How much help are the boys?"

"Chris, you got kids?"

I shook my head.

"Then I'll forgive you for that question. They're worthless. I was holding it to keep peace in the family."

"Going to rebuild?"

"Excellent question, my friend. Don't know."

"Were you at the fire?"

"I wasn't even in South Carolina, was at, umm, a meeting in Atlanta. I didn't know anything about it until the next day."

"That had to be a shock."

Another sip later, he said, "I probably shouldn't say it, but I'm glad it's gone. The insurance money will help clear some debts. With that said, I feel bad for my tenants."

"Have they found places to live?"

"The only one I've seen since the fire is a kid who works at Bert's. He said he's living in his car."

"That's rough."

"He's young, will be okay."

I remembered how Cindy said he'd been vague about the meeting he allegedly was attending and where he stayed in Atlanta.

"I haven't been to Atlanta in years. All I remember is construction downtown. Traffic was always disrupted. Is it still that way?"

"Don't know. I was a few miles from downtown."

Hadn't Cindy said the meeting was at a downtown hotel? I also couldn't figure a way to ask if he torched the building. Even if I had, I didn't get a chance. He looked at his watch for the third time since I sat down.

"Better get home. My wife will be calling out the police if I don't show up soon. Thanks for the beer, Chris. Nice meeting you."

He slid off the chair and was out the door before I paid his tab. I not only bought his second beer, but the first was also on me.

Barb probably passed Russell on the way down the stairs. She arrived with a smile and proclaiming that she was starved, a common occurrence, or so it seems. The crowd had thinned so we had a choice of three tables. We ordered then Barb told me about her day, the closing-time rush, then a story about a customer who wanted Barb to gift wrap a dozen books he was giving to his three children. He eventually bought the books but was disappointed she didn't gift wrap.

I started to tell about meeting Russell O'Leary, but her body language told me she didn't want to talk about the fire. We found much more pleasant topics to enjoy with our meal. After supper, I walked her across the street to her condo, where our pleasant topics continued.

Chapter Twenty-Seven

Barb had kept my mind off the fire for several hours, but the next morning, I couldn't shake what Russell had said about being glad the building burned, and his comment about not being in downtown Atlanta. Had I misunderstood what Cindy shared about his meeting? A phone call would be a simple way to find out.

"Morning, Chief."

"Are you on your way to the Dog?"

"No, but I can be. Why?"

"Because if you're not here, how can you buy me breakfast."

"See you in a few minutes."

"Don't you love it when a plan comes together?" she said, then hung up.

The temperature was beginning to feel like Christmas, so I drove rather than walked. My half-hearted exercise plan would have to wait. There was a rare empty parking space in front of the restaurant, reducing my exercise by more steps.

Cindy was at a table in the center of the room. As I made my way over, she motioned for a server to bring a second cup of coffee.

"I thought you'd be home fixing bacon, eggs, hash browns, and toast for Rose, Luke, and Larry," I said, knowing that'd be the last thing she'd be doing.

"You've been hanging around Noelle Ward too long. She's the fiction writer."

I was surprised she knew Noelle. "Why did you mention Noelle?"

"She said she knew you."

"Where'd you meet her?"

"Did you forget there was a big-ass fire at her building?"

"No, but—"

"She stopped by the office yesterday. Said something about telling you about seeing someone nosing around the apartment. You said if she saw the guy again to call you, so you could tell me, or something like that."

My coffee arrived. Cindy interrupted her story to tell the server what she wanted for breakfast. I exhibited as much originality as I usually do when I ordered French toast.

"Your new writer friend said instead of dragging you in the middle of something that was none of your business, she told me directly about the guy who'd creeped her out."

I took a sip of coffee, then said, "Is that how Noelle said it?"

Cindy smiled. "I added none of your business."

"I figured. Did she give you anything that'd help find the guy?"

"Nothing that wouldn't describe a third of the population. I told her to call me—I repeat, call me—if she sees him again."

"Good plan."

"Chris, if memory serves me correct, you called me. Any particular reason other than to raise my blood pressure?"

"Didn't you tell me Russell O'Leary was in Atlanta the day of the fire?"

She took a small notebook out of her coat pocket, flipped through a few pages, then said, "The owner of a pile of charcoal said he was attending a get-rich-quick rip-off seminar in downtown Atlanta. He didn't say rip-off, that's my astute analysis of the hotel-meeting-room con-artist seminar."

"Are you sure he said downtown Atlanta?"

She flipped another page. "Said the seminar was at the Westin Peachtree Plaza, downtown Atlanta. Why did someone see him here?"

"I met him last night at Loggerhead's."

She shook her head. "Let me guess, you were minding your own business nibbling on a fry when low-and-behold Russell popped up out of nowhere and introduced himself."

"Close. I thought it was him, so I introduced myself."

"While minding your own business, I'm sure. Moving right along, why ask about Atlanta?"

Breakfast arrived. I poured syrup on the French toast, then said, "He told me he'd stayed a few miles outside downtown Atlanta."

"Pray tell, how did that come up in the conversation?" Cindy asked, then took a bite of toast.

"You'd told me he was in downtown Atlanta, so I said how bad construction had been the last time I was there. Asked if it was still bad."

Cindy rolled her eyes. "Chris, have you been to Atlanta since Sherman burned it?"

"Not quite that long ago."

"Charles must be learnin' you private detective techniques for tricking suspects. Did he say anything else about his trip?"

"Not about the trip, but said he was glad the building burned. Insurance would let him pay off debts."

"Suppose you would've already mentioned it if he told you he set the fire?"

"Chief, you would've been the first to know."

"Do you think he did?"

I shrugged. "Told me he wasn't good at maintaining the building; he hated getting called at all hours about problems; he threw out he wasn't fond of dealing with tenants. He didn't say it, but as you shared, he was behind on the mortgage."

"Does that mean you think he did it?"

"Cindy, I talked to the man for fifteen minutes. He seemed like a nice guy, but who knows. It bothers me he'd either lie to you or to me about where he was in Georgia, especially when it didn't matter one way or the other to me."

"And, he said he was glad the building burned."

I smiled. "That too."

"I suppose I'd better have another talk with the confused, former landlord."

"Sounds like the chiefly thing to do."

The server returned with refills on our drinks. Cindy took a sip of the refreshed coffee, then said, "Ho, Ho, Ho!"

"How are you and Larry adjusting to houseguests?"

"Larry hasn't been home enough to know they're there.

When he gets home, he's so exhausted he flops in bed not acknowledging any of us. Sort of pleasant. Luke is still spending several hours a day at the store. He told me last night, Larry made him, how did he put it, umm, vice president of Christmas sales. It thrilled the heck out of the kid. I figure it was Larry's way of not giving Luke more money."

"How about Rose?"

"Fine most of the time."

"Most of the time?"

"Her a-hole ex keeps calling. It screws up her mood every time."

"What's he want?"

"What do you think? Wants her to come crawling back to Morristown."

"She thinking about it?"

"The first Thursday after hell freezes over."

"Good."

Cindy stuffed a bite of egg in her mouth, then mumbled, "Yep."

Chapter Twenty-Eight

An hour after breakfast with Cindy the phone rang. Her name appeared on the screen.

"Didn't get enough of me at breakfast?" I said.

"I'm beginning to see why you detest caller ID. How many favors have you asked me for since we've met?"

"The exact number?"

"Never mind. It's a zillion, give or take."

"Sounds right," I said, wondering where the conversation was headed.

"How many have I asked you for?"

"Way fewer than a zillion."

"How about fewer than three?"

"Close."

"I figure you owe me a few, quite a few."

"Cindy, you have a favor to ask?"

"Wow, you're smarter than the average bonehead I deal with."

"Flattery is not one of your strengths," I said, then chuckled. "What do you need?"

"Since Rose has been at the house, I've spent less time with her than I've spent with the town drunk. Luke has been at the hardware store every day, but I know how tired of Larry someone can become. Plus, how many AA batteries can a nine-year-old put in bags before his battery runs down?"

"Your point?"

"Rose told me Luke has been wanting to eat at Planet Follywood, so today she's taking him there for lunch. Think you could miraculously happen in about the time they're arriving? I think conversation with someone other than the television would be good for Rose. Luke seems to like you. Heck if I know why."

"There you go with flattery again. When are they going?"

"I'm guessing noon, but Rose didn't say."

"I'll be there."

"Great. I would say I owe you one, but since you're a zillion favors behind, I'll leave it at thanks."

Planet Follywood was at the intersection of East Erie Avenue and Center Street and was one of Folly's most-established restaurants. It's also known for a large mural painted on the side of the building featuring larger-than-life paintings of Hollywood icons including John Wayne, Marilyn Monroe, Sammy Davis Jr, Elvis, plus a few others.

I arrived ten minutes before noon and stood across the street where I could see diners entering the restaurant. I wasn't there long; my intended targets arrived before noon. Luke pulled his mom past the entry where he pointed at the mural. Rose smiled then escorted her son to the door. I gave them a couple of minutes to settle before I "miraculously" entered.

The interior looked like what I imagine beach restaurants and bars looked like in days gone by. Luke and the food were probably the newest things in there. It was apparent why Planet Follywood was popular with residents and vacationers who wanted to relive their past. Neon beer signs were attached to most walls; another mural was painted on the concrete block wall to the left; wood paneling covered another wall and the ceiling. Overall, a warm, welcoming feel permeated the room. Luke and his mom were seated at a bar-height table in front of the mural and across from a Christmas tree. Luke wore a red sweatshirt that looked like it'd just come out of the package. It probably had. Rose had on a starched, white blouse and a tan lightweight jacket.

Luke spotted me standing in the entry. He waved then said something to his mom. She turned and waved me over.

"Hi, Chris, having lunch?"

I told her I was, then Luke said, "Want to sit with us?"

"I don't want to intrude," although, of course, I did.

"Nonsense," Rose said, "have a seat."

Luke watched me sit. "Been in here before?"

"Many times," I said. "How about you?"

"Our first," Rose answered for her son. "Luke's been talking about it since he saw the mural on the wall outside."

"Cool," he said. "Mom said all those people were in movies, like old movies."

"It was painted by a man from Charleston named James Christopher Hill."

"Think it was okay for him to paint all over that wall? I'd get in trouble if I did something like that."

"I'm sure he had permission."

A server arrived and took our drink orders.

The server left. Luke pointed at the Christmas tree. "Cool tree."

Guess we'd talked enough about the mural.

I said, "It is neat."

"Mom and me put up a tree in Aunt Cindy and Uncle Larry's living room."

Rose touched Luke's arm. "Mom and I."

Luke rolled his eyes, and said, "Mr. Landrum, never marry an English professor."

I smiled. "I'll keep that in mind."

The server returned with our drinks, saving Luke from more English lessons. She asked if we were ready to order. Rose said we needed a few more minutes. Luke took over the conversation from that point, telling me about working at the hardware store, about how cool his bedroom was, how he could see the Folly River and the marsh out his window, and several other things that were important to him but which I forgot as soon as he finished mentioning them. Rose sat back and watched her son share his day to day, almost moment to moment experiences.

The server tried again to see if we were ready to order. Rose asked Luke if he was. He turned to the server and asked if they had hot dogs. They did, so he ordered one, Rose stuck with a cheeseburger, and I ordered a chicken finger basket. Rose excused herself and headed to the restroom.

Luke watched her go, leaned close to me, then said, "Mr. Landrum, think you could do something for me?"

"Suppose it depends on what?"

"I want to get Mom something nice for Christmas. I

heard you could find teeth from old, dead sharks on the beach. Can you believe that?"

I nodded.

Luke looked toward the restrooms, turned to me, and said, "Someone who came in the store said people make jewelry from the teeth. Do they sell them somewhere here?"

"In fact, they do. Barb's Books has several pieces of shark tooth jewelry made by Michelle, a local artist."

"Could you buy a necklace with a shark tooth on it for me to give Mom? If it's not too expensive. I have money Uncle Larry paid me for working, so I can pay you back."

"I'll be glad to."

He again glanced toward the restroom. "I'd also like to get one for Aunt Cindy. She's been nice to us."

"I'll do that, Luke."

"Make Aunt Cindy's a little cheaper than the one for Mom. I want Mom to know she's number one."

I smiled and said I would. "What about Uncle Larry?"

"All he wants for Christmas is to sleep for two days without being interrupted or hearing his cash register ding. I'm going to give him a quiet house. No TV, no playing loud."

"That's a great gift."

"What are you two men plotting out here?" Rose said as she returned to the table.

"Nothing, Mom. Guy talk."

"Luke, why don't you go wash your hands before our food arrives?"

He sighed, then slid off the chair.

"Rose, you have a great kid."

"Most of the time."

"Have you told Cindy about Kenneth's visit?"

"No."

"It's none of my business, but I think you should. I know you disagree, but he'd be a prime suspect in starting the fire. Cindy would have a good chance of learning if he was here the day of the fire. Don't you want to know?"

"Yes, but I don't want her going ballistic."

"Rose, I've known your sister a long time. She's at her best when faced with difficult situations. I'd trust her with my life. You can trust her with the truth."

Luke returned wiping his hands together. He smiled, then said, "What are you two grownups plotting out here?"

Touché.

Our conspiring ended when the food arrived. We spent the next hour enjoying the food, the eclectic restaurant, and each other. Cindy was right. Rose and Luke left the restaurant in better spirits and more relaxed than when they arrived. So did I.

Chapter Twenty-Nine

I headed to Barb's Books after leaving Rose and Luke full of food and smiles. A woman I didn't recognize was perusing the romance section while Barb was behind the counter thumbing through a book. She was wearing one of her signature red blouses and black slacks. She saw me at the door, closed the book, and smiled.

"What brings you in? I know it's not to buy a book."

"Right again," I said, then moved to a small table near the check-out counter that was covered with a white velour cloth. "I'm not looking for a book but a couple of these." On the velour, there were several silver necklaces, a couple of bracelets, plus five sets of earrings, all featuring black, shark teeth.

"Christopher, if I may be so bold, I suggest if you're looking to buy jewelry for a woman, you may not want to shop in a store owned by the lady you're dating."

I laughed. "I'll file that wise advice. Actually, I'm

Christmas shopping for a gentleman I know." I then shared my assignment.

"In that case," Barb said, "I think these earrings would be perfect for our Chief." Barb held one up to her ear. It had a half-inch long shark tooth dangling from the short chain. "First, they're pretty. Second, they could visually communicate to local miscreants not to mess with the Chief."

"Perfect. How about Rose?"

She modeled three necklaces before we agreed on one that not only had a shark tooth but a small, silver heart. She asked if I wanted her to gift-wrap the gifts.

"Didn't think you gift-wrapped."

She looked at the customer browsing in the romance section, then said, "I don't unless it's for someone special, someone like Luke."

"Or for me?"

"Nope. I'll also give your young friend the family discount."

I thanked her for the discount, to which she said she wasn't doing it for me, but for Luke. I told her about having lunch at Cindy's suggestion with Rose and Luke. She said she was glad Rose was getting out, hoping it'd keep her from thinking about the fire or losing most everything. I told her how I'd suggested, again, that she tell her sister about her ex-husband's visit to Folly the day before the fire.

"Speaking of fire victims," Barb said as she reached under the counter to pull out a roll of red and gold wrapping paper, "Noelle was in an hour ago. She's off work this week. Said without having an apartment to hang out in, she didn't know what to do with her time. She was heading to the library to work on her book."

"How's she doing?"

"She's young, adapts fairly well to adversity. Better than I would."

I shared what Noelle told me about thinking someone was watching her.

"She told me."

"Think she's right?"

Barb shrugged. "No way to know."

The browser carried a stack of books to the counter. Barb rang them up, then thanked the shopper, who left the store heavier than when she arrived.

Barb finished wrapping the gifts, waved off my attempt to pay, then said, "Let me bounce an idea off you. Noelle seems like a nice woman. She's funny, has a responsible job in Charleston, shows a huge amount of initiative with the book she's writing."

"I agree."

"I hate seeing her living out of her truck. I've got a spare bedroom going to waste. What do you think about me offering to let her stay in my condo until she finds the kind of apartment she's looking for?" Barb laughed. "The perfect dump she calls her dream apartment."

"Are you comfortable with it?"

"I'm leaning that way."

"I think it's a great idea, as long as you're comfortable."

———

That night began with me alternating between wondering if Rose would finally tell her sister about her ex-husband's visit, and my thoughts about Barb asking Noelle to move in with her.

My mind shifted to wondering who'd started the fire. Regardless of what Rose thought, I could see it being her ex. He could be eliminated if he was in Tennessee on the day of the fire. Ty could also have made Aimee's fiancée angry enough to start the fire. Most likely, he would've or could've known Ty was at work, so the fire was set to make a point rather than to harm Ty. That brought me to Horace, Janice's ex-husband. She was convinced he's the culprit, but it seems like a stretch. He'd moved on, although Janice's attorney was still after him for money. Was that reason enough to burn her building?

Neil's former boss had more than enough reason to want revenge for being turned in to the IRS. It'd been some time since Neil did that, so would he still be angry enough to set the fire? Then what about the customer Neil had unceremoniously thrown out of the bar? Granted, the man threatened Neil, but, as Cal said, that wasn't uncommon, and seldom led to anything. Could this be the exception?

Noelle was convinced someone was following her, or at least, keeping an eye on her, plus someone left her the note. Without knowing why there was no way to determine if she bothered someone enough to torch the building.

The most logical arsonist was Russell O'Leary. He was behind in his mortgage, appeared to have little means to catch up. His alibi for the time of the fire was suspect at best. Finally, he'd told me he didn't want the building in the first place.

From my limited time with Russell, he appeared to be a nice man, yet was in over his head maintaining the building. The fire was set when the building most likely would've been vacant. That seemed like something Russell would've taken into consideration.

Cindy knew everything I did about Russell, so I was confident she was following up. So, with all of that cleared up, I should be able to get a good night's sleep.

So, why didn't I?

Chapter Thirty

Despite little sleep, I was awake at six o'clock. I closed my eyes attempting to catch a few more minutes sleep. I failed. The next thing I knew, it was eight-thirty, far more than a few minutes later. While well-rested, I was hungry. The unseasonably warm weather from a few days ago had returned, so I walked next door. Ty was at the register adjusting a string of Christmas lights attached around the check-out stand.

"Hey, Mr. Landrum, want a treat?"

"No thanks, Ty. I wanted to stop by to see how you were doing."

"I'm doing better than these lights, Mr. Landrum."

"You're brighter than they are," I said. He could take it any way he wanted. "How's Lost?"

"Great. That little critter loves the warmer weather. She isn't a fan of staying in the car but handles it good when the temperature ain't too cold."

I nodded, thinking that'd apply to all of us.

Ty continued, "Anything I can help you with?"

"No. Grabbing coffee and something for breakfast."

"You know where it is. Merry Christmas."

"You going to Cal's Christmas party?"

"I don't know. I'll be working Bert's free community breakfast. It's over at ten, so I don't know if I'll be here longer than that. Besides, ain't most of the people at Cal's party old, umm, older than me?"

"All ages will be there," I said, although on average age he was right. "I'd love to see you."

"I'll ponder it," he said, then started waiting on a man who'd arrived at the counter.

I grabbed a cinnamon Danish, drew a cup of coffee, then returned to the register.

Ty took my money and said, "Done pondered it, Mr. Landrum. If I get out of here early enough, I'll be there."

"Fantastic."

I started home, smiled when I saw Ty's Miata in the back of the small parking lot, then jumped out of the way when an older-model white Chevrolet Malibu with a dent in the driver's door pulled in, nearly hitting me.

Janice Raque stepped out, gave me a dirty look like I had some nerve getting in the way of her car, hesitated, then smiled.

"Sorry, Chris. Didn't recognize you."

I wondered if that meant she wouldn't be sorry if she'd run down anyone else.

"Hi, Janice."

"Glad I ran into you." She smiled. "Didn't mean literally. Got something to tell you. Got a minute?"

I told her I did.

Her arms were wrapped around her torso like she was cold. "Let's get in the car? It's warmer."

I wasn't cold but agreed. Since she had something to say, I remained quiet and took a sip of coffee.

"Remember the other day when we were talking? I told you I was certain Horace was the one who set the fire."

That wasn't something I could easily forget. "Yes."

"Wasn't him."

"How do you know?"

"We had, guess still have, a mutual friend. Name's Sally. She called yesterday to see if I'd heard about Horace. I'd heard a bunch of things about the no-good, two-timing, goat herder. I wasn't sure what she was talking about, so I asked. You'll never guess what she told me."

She hesitated. I wondered if she wanted me to guess. Instead, I said, "What?"

"He had a stroke, happened two days before the fire. The two-timer was in the hospital in Mt. Pleasant. Nearly kicked the bucket."

"That's too bad."

She sighed. "Not bad enough. He didn't die. Got released yesterday. That's what Sally called to tell me. Like she thought I cared. No sir, I didn't."

"He couldn't have started the fire."

"I figured the stroke was caused by the old man pretending he was a youngster fiddlin' with that floozy he ran off with if you know what I mean." She offered a sly grin.

I did. Scratch one suspect. Which reminded me of something that'd bothered me since I had lunch with her in Snapper Jack's, something that contributed to me getting little sleep last night. It was something she said before nearly falling off the chair. Instead of following up at the time, I thought it better to catch her before she hit the floor.

"Janice, remember when we met the other day in Snapper Jack's?"

She smiled. "Not much. I was a bit under the weather if you know what I mean."

Drunk would have been the word I would've chosen.

"We were talking about the apartment building and you said people had asked you about living there. You mentioned two people, a man, I believe his name was Jeff, and a woman named something like Kaycee. Remember?"

"I remember them, but don't remember telling you. Sure it was me?"

Her not remembering didn't surprise me considering her condition at the time.

"What do you remember about them?"

"The guy, Jeff, or something like that, looked like a street person if you ask me. He stopped me in the parking lot one afternoon, said he was looking for somewhere to live and wanted to know what I thought about the apartment building. I told him I didn't think much of it, but that's about all."

"What about the woman? You started to tell me something, but, umm, we were interrupted." I didn't add, "by you falling off the chair."

"Let's see. I believe she said her name was Kaycee Ericson. She came knocking on my door, suppose a week or so before the fire." Janice closed her eyes, then tapped her fingers on the steering wheel. "Told me she owned some apartments. They were full and she had someone she was looking for a place to live. Think I told her about the vacant unit on the first floor. She then asked how long I lived there.

If I liked living in the building. Then she asked how many people lived in my apartment. That got my dander up. I asked if she was a census taker or what. I wanted to find out if she was something official before I told her it was none of her damned business who lived in my apartment. Nearly slammed the door in her face." She could tell I was getting pissed." Janice looked out the side window, scratched the side of her face, then said, "She then told me she was looking at buying the place. That got my attention, so I let her in, offered her a beer, told her everything she wanted to know. Even told her about the leaky faucet, although I didn't have to since she could hear it drip, drip, drip all the way in the living room. Figured if she bought it, she couldn't be as bad a landlord as O'Leary. Our conversation then headed a direction I didn't like."

"How?"

"She started whispering like there were other people in the room nosing into what she was saying. Said she was trying to figure if she could fix the building up enough so she could increase rents enough to make the deal work." She looked at me and shrugged. "Didn't think it was too wise telling a tenant all that. I'm no math wizard, but it sounded like it would've had me digging deeper in my pocketbook to live there. Hell, Chris, if I could afford a higher rent, I wouldn't have been living in that dump."

"Janice, did she give you a card or her contact information?"

"Sure did."

"Do you have it?"

She frowned and looked at her hand on the steering wheel. "It was in the apartment." She clapped her hands together like she was wiping something off. "It's ashes."

"Janice, I appreciate you sharing. I don't want to keep you any longer."

"Chris, you ain't keeping me. All I have to do is go back to the damned hotel room."

"I'd better be going anyway. Are you going to be at Cal's Christmas party?"

She nodded. "Anything to get out of the hotel room."

Chapter Thirty-One

I finally made it home and to the cinnamon Danish I'd been carrying for a half hour. I microwaved the cold coffee then sat at the kitchen table. It was good eliminating Horace from the suspect list, although I never had him near the top.

Janice did say something that struck me as significant, more than anything about Horace. That was Kaycee Ericson's visit to Janice's apartment a week before the fire. She apparently was someone who wanted to buy the building. Was Russell O'Leary going to sell to her? I'd never heard of Kaycee Ericson until Janice shared her name. Was she local?

A call to Chief LaMond might provide answers.

"What do you want now?" she said.

I'd given up long ago trying to get my friends to answer with anything resembling a civil response.

"What do you know about Kaycee Ericson?"

"Chris, you've been around Charles way too much. What's Kaycee have to do with anything?"

I shared what Janice Raque had told me about the visit.

"Interesting. Are you trying to screw up my theory that O'Leary torched his building?"

"Cindy, you're Chief. I'm simply a lowly citizen sharing a story. I have no business sticking my nose in your investigation."

"Chris, I say this lovingly, you're as full of crap as Dumbo the elephant."

"Glad you said it lovingly."

"Want to pout or learn about Kaycee?"

"What do you think?"

"She lives in a condo across from Harris Teeter. Been here two years at the most. Someone said she moved from New Jersey, is connected to money. She's built a couple of new oceanfront McMansions, sold them for a tidy profit."

"How do you know all that?"

"I'm Chief. I know everything."

I waited, knowing once she got past the bluster, she'd elaborate.

"She's been all the talk around City Hall. With the two McMansions and now a condo building she wants to develop out West Ashley near the County Park, she's good at pushing the zoning regulation boundaries. So far, she hasn't crossed the line, but according to folks who know more about zoning than this lowly public servant, she's within millimeters of violating the regs."

"Cindy, is this enough for you to talk with Kaycee?"

"To be determined."

"Meaning?"

"Meaning, in fifteen minutes after I get a pesky citizen off the phone, Russell O'Leary will be in this big impressive office of Director of Public Safety. It's time for me to ram sharpened bamboo sticks under his fingernails to get the truth about his alleged visit to the metropolis of Atlanta. Truth like where he stayed, how long he was actually there, and if he's fortunate, proof he was there instead of here incinerating his building."

"Cindy, other than bamboo under his nails, that sounds like a good plan. Will you add questions about him selling the building?"

"Wasn't until three minutes ago. Bye."

Progress, she said bye before hanging up.

Thirty minutes later, the phone rang. At first, I thought it was Cindy, then realized she'd be talking to Russell. The screen read *Barb*.

"Good morning, my favorite bookstore owner."

"Only bookstore owner."

"You're my favorite, regardless how many bookstores there are. What did I do to deserve a call?"

"Nothing. I wanted to tell you something I did last night."

That got my attention. "What?"

"Invited Noelle to move in with me until she finds the kind of apartment she's looking for."

"That's wonderful. What did she say?"

"Short version, yes. Slightly longer version, she was thrilled. She said if she had to spend many more nights in her truck, she'd either have to find a chiropractor or a witch doctor to work on her back. Before she told me that, she kept saying she didn't want to inconvenience me. I told her she wouldn't. She kept offering to pay rent. I told her no. I couldn't tell for certain because of her sunglasses, but I think I saw tears."

"You're a kind person. She's lucky to have you as a friend."

"Don't know about that, but it made me feel good being able to help."

"The Christmas spirit in action."

"'Tis the season. I met her at Loggerhead's. Before she left, know what she said?"

"I hope it was thank you."

Barb laughed. "She got serious, touched me on the arm, looked across the street at my condo building, and said something like, 'Don't take offense, Barb. Your condo is way too nice for what I'm looking for.' I told her I wasn't offended. She's moving in tonight."

I was touched by Barb's generosity. After her call, I got up from the table, carried my coffee cup to my office. Charles was right, all that was in the room was a small table holding my computer and printer, a chair, and a filing cabinet holding years of tax papers, plus other items I probably didn't need to save.

I sat, took a sip of coffee getting cold again, and punched in Neil Wilson's number. I didn't think he was going to answer, but he finally did. He sounded like the phone awakened him. It may have. I told him who was calling then asked if he was available for lunch. He said he was due at Cal's at three but could meet me at the Lost Dog Cafe in an hour.

Good to his word, he was standing in front of the restaurant when I arrived. He looked like he'd just climbed out of bed, although I knew he'd been awake an hour earlier. He wore a royal blue sweatshirt with The Griffon Pub in large block letters on the front, tan slacks with fraying cuffs. His hair was sticking out from a Charleston RiverDogs cap. He looked like he'd slept in his clothes.

We were escorted to a table in the center of the room. There were only four other tables occupied. Neil put his hat on the edge of the table, yawned, and ran his hand through his hair. It did little to get hairs going the same direction.

"Did you work last night?"

"Until two this morning. Can't you tell?"

I smiled. "Yes."

A server, who said her name was Anna, appeared with pen in hand.

"Coffee," Neil said. "That'll get my eyes open enough to read the menu."

I told her the same.

I filled the time until Anna returned by talking about the near-countless photos of dogs adorning the walls. Neil observed how different the decorations and colors were from those in Cal's. Anna returned with mugs of steaming hot coffee. She said she'd be back to take our order. Neil took three sips before speaking.

"I appreciate you calling," he said, then hesitated, "although it made me wonder why."

Good to her word, Anna returned asking if we were ready to order. While I'd told Neil the invitation was for lunch, he had breakfast on his mind. He started to order a bagel until I said I was buying. He switched to bacon and eggs; I went with French toast, surprise, surprise. Anna said, "Excellent choices," and headed to the kitchen. I wondered if she ever said, "Terrible choice."

"Chris, I appreciate you picking up the tab. Staying at the hotel is breaking me."

"That's what I wanted to talk to you about. I have an

extra room at my place. If you want, you could move in until you find somewhere of your own."

He stared at me. "You're kidding."

"It's nothing luxurious. The room's small. Has a blowup mattress, no real bed."

Okay, it doesn't have a blowup mattress, but with luck, it will before he gets there.

"Not to be unappreciative," he said, "how much?"

"Nothing. It's yours until you find a place to stay."

He repeated, "You're kidding."

"I'm serious."

He stood, walked around the table, and shook my hand. "Thank you. I can't believe something good is happening to me at Christmas."

Anna arrived with our food, so Neil returned to his chair.

He took a bite of eggs, then said, "I won't be able to move in until tomorrow. Besides, I've already paid the hotel for tonight. Wouldn't want that money to go to waste."

Good. That'll give me time to find a blowup mattress.

"That's fine, Neil."

Two more bites and he said, "Chris, you're really not kidding?"

Chapter Thirty-Two

Before leaving the Dog, Neil told me he needed to get to the hotel to take a shower before heading to work. He wanted to use as much of the hotel's water as he could to get his money's worth. I remained at the table to call Charles.

"Ready to go?" I said.

"Sure," he said, not asking where.

"I'll be there in ten minutes." I hung up on him, a move he'd perfected. It felt good being on this end of the line for a change.

Ten minutes later, I pulled in his crushed shell and gravel parking lot to see him standing in front of his apartment. He was wearing a maroon Texas A&M sweatshirt under a lightweight jacket, well-worn jeans, and his Tilley.

"We going to buy my Christmas present?" he said as he slid in the passenger seat.

"No," I said, then pulled out of the lot.

He snapped his fingers. "Done figured it out. We're going to catch a flight to Bora Bora for the holidays?"

"No," I repeated. This was nearly as much fun as hanging up on him.

We'd pulled off the island and past Harris Teeter.

"I see we're not grocery shopping. You can fill in our destination at any time."

Five minutes later, I pulled in Walmart's parking lot.

"Let me guess," he said, "we're going to Walmart."

"I see why you think you're a detective."

Before he could respond with one of his many smart-aleck remarks, the phone rang.

"Good afternoon, Cindy."

I parked and Charles motioned for me to put the phone on speaker. Rather than having to repeat everything she said, I tapped the speaker icon. Charles smiled.

"It's getting better by the minute," Cindy said. "Don't be surprised the next few days if you hear Russell O'Leary has been arrested for torching his apartment building."

"He confess?"

"It's not what he told me but what he didn't."

Charles leaned toward the phone. "What's that mean, Chief?"

"Chris, you done gone and got a talking disease. You sound like your worthless friend."

Charles said, "Chief, he doesn't sound anything like Bob Howard."

I heard her chuckle before saying, "His other worthless friend."

Enough! "Chief, what did Russell tell you?"

"He stuck to his story that sounds like a fairytale. Still claims he was in Atlanta, as in downtown Atlanta, attending a get-rich-quick seminar, sleeping in a nearby cheap hotel, paying cash, and not able to remember the name of where he stayed. His body language and failure to look me in the eyes made me not believe a word of it."

Charles said, "Who wouldn't want to look in such a lovely lady's eyes? He's definitely lying."

"Charles, your BS is appreciated, but it doesn't prove guilt."

"Cindy," I said, "if that's the case, why do you think he'll be arrested?"

"The only thing he appeared certain of in his far-fetched version of a trip to Atlanta, was where the seminar was held. After he left, I called the Westin Peachtree Plaza, the hotel he could remember. I had a pleasant talk with a nice lady with a cute southern accent. Seems she's in charge of meetings and seminars."

"Let me guess," I said, "there wasn't a get-rich-quick seminar the day of the apartment fire."

"Not that day, not the day before, not the day after, in fact, not the week before or after. The closest thing they hosted was a two-day meeting on financing options for large office buildings held two days after Russell returned to South Carolina."

Charles said, "So why isn't he sitting in a jail cell?"

"Charged with what, fibbing to the fuzz? We need more. I told him to bring proof, anything, gas receipts, restaurant receipts, hell, I'd even take a receipt written on toilet paper from a panhandler if Russell donated to the bum's liquor fund. Otherwise, my hands are tied until I have something more than a hunch to arrest him on."

"Cindy," I said, "you're convinced he did it?"

"Plum near a thousand percent."

"Have you talked to Kaycee Ericson?"

"I'm calling her as soon as I get off the phone with Folly's nosiest troublemakers."

It didn't take Charles's detective skills to know who she was talking about. I wished her luck.

"Did you drive me out here to sit in the parking lot?" Charles said after Cindy ended her call with the troublemakers.

Instead of telling him where we were going, I took the show him approach. It took several unsuccessful trips up aisles before I found the blowup mattresses in the sports and outdoors section. I savored the walk by not telling him what I was trying to find. Cruel, but sweet revenge for him doing similar things over the years.

I finally gave in and shared why I was looking at blowup mattresses.

"Wonderful. You took my advice about taking in Neil."

He'd suggested it, but I hated giving him the satisfaction of knowing he was right. Oh well, why not? After all, it's Christmas.

"Yes, it was your idea, a good one."

He beamed and curtsied. It was worth telling him the truth to see him happy. We studied our options when he came up with another good idea. I should buy an electric pump to inflate the mattress. It was a good idea, but he didn't have to add I'd need the pump because I was too old to blow it up with my fossilizing lungs.

On the way home, I called Bob Howard and hit the speaker button for Charles. While I had confidence Cindy was on the right trail with Russell, and that she'd contact Kaycee Ericson like she told me she would, I wasn't ready to convict the landlord. He seemed sincere with everything he'd told me. It also seemed counterproductive when he told me he was glad the building had been reduced to ashes. If anyone had dirt on or would know someone who would know anything bad about Kaycee, it'd be Bob.

Willie Nelson was singing "On the Road Again" in the background, when Bob answered with, "On your way to get a cheeseburger?"

"No."

"Then why are you wasting my valuable time?"

"Bob, I appreciate you taking time out of your busy day to talk to me," I said, exuding sarcasm.

"Damned right, I'm busy. You know how much energy it takes to sit, drink a beer, and watch the overpaid cook fixing burgers? What do you need?"

See why we're such good friends?

"What do you know about Kaycee Ericson?"

"You nosin' in something that's none of your business?"

"Yes."

"Figures. Don't know much. She's bought a few buildings over here, hear she's itching to be a big-time developer. Heard she either is or was married to Alan, who actually is a big-time developer. That's it, my well of information's dry."

"Thanks."

"Does this have something to do with the apartment building fire?"

"Yes."

"Think she set it?"

"Maybe."

"Let me make some calls to guys who'll know more about her than what I said."

"Bob, I'd appreciate it."

"Don't appreciate it enough to frequent this fine-dining establishment." He hung up.

I was impressed, first because Bob gave me some information without me having to buy food, and second, Charles hadn't interrupted.

Chapter Thirty-Three

After dropping Charles at his apartment, I went home to repurpose my office into a bedroom. I was glad Charles encouraged me to buy the pump, otherwise, it would've taken me five years and probably a heart attack to inflate the mattress with lung power. Using the pump, I had the bed inflated, covered with sheets that were too large, and added a pillow I'd forgotten I had. All Neil's bedroom lacked was a piece of chocolate on the pillow and a Gideon's Bible.

With my hotelier duties completed, I moved to the living room to review what, if anything, I'd learned during the extraordinarily busy day. Since I'd innocently walked to Bert's for breakfast and coffee, I'd talked with Ty, Janice, and Neil, residents of sixty percent of the five occupied apartments in the ill-fated building. Janice eliminated Horace as a suspect, while adding Kaycee. Two of the displaced residents, Noelle and Neil, had found somewhere to live. And, it appeared another suspect, Russell, was on the verge of being arrested.

While a lot had transpired, I wasn't closer to figuring out who set the fire than I'd been on my walk to Bert's. My phone rang as I came to that realization.

Charles said, "I'll pick you up at nine in the morning."

"Going to buy my Christmas present, or taking a flight to Bora Bora?"

Silence was the response to what I thought was a humorous comment. He'd hung up.

Charles's definition of nine o'clock was eight-thirty, so I was waiting for him on my screened-in porch when he pulled in the drive.

"On time, good," he said as I slipped in the car.

He wore a navy-blue sweatshirt with Auburn University in orange on the front.

"Morning, Charles," I said, and resisted asking where we were going.

He drove two blocks then turned on East Arctic Avenue, before saying, "Know why I wore this sweatshirt?"

"To keep you warm?" I said, knowing it wasn't the answer he wanted.

"Guess again."

Then it struck me.

"Auburn has a well-known college of veterinarian medicine, so we're going to Martha Wright's zoo."

His head jerked my direction. "Wow! I may give you a promotion in my private detective agency."

"Charles, now that I know where we're going, how about why?"

"Martha called last night. Asked if I could stop by this morning."

"Why?"

"Suppose because of my charm, good looks, way with women."

I rolled my eyes. "Again, why?"

"Clueless. I'm bringing you in case she got a stray mountain lion."

I didn't waste time saying the mountain lion theory was as remote as her wanting him to visit because of his good looks, charm, and way with women.

Martha greeted us at the door. I was surprised no barking dogs were surrounding her.

"Glad you could make it," she said. "I see you brought Chris."

She was smiling so I couldn't tell what she thought about Charles's plus one.

"Chris loves hearing about your animals, so I thought he'd enjoy visiting."

I did?

"Great," she said, with little enthusiasm. "Come in. We're gathered in the sitting room."

Other than Squeezy, I didn't know who "we" could include. Seconds later, that mystery was answered when I saw Martha's neighbor, Dixie Thompson, seated in one of the wingback chairs. I'd met Dixie before meeting Martha. She lived across the street from Martha and had been her friend for years. She was in her late-seventies, five-foot-eight, thin, with white hair that would put the whitest paint color to shame. Her hair looked even whiter compared to her tanned, leathery face.

Dixie stood, held up a tumbler holding an amber-colored liquid, and said, "Moscow."

Charles was the invited guest, so I let him respond, besides, I had no idea what to say.

"Huh?" he articulately said.

Dixie held the tumbler higher. "It's five o'clock somewhere."

Martha laughed. "In Moscow."

"Oh," Charles said.

Watching Dixie sway as she chuckled at Martha's remark, I wondered where it'd been five o'clock an hour or two earlier.

"Fellas," Martha said, "how about a hot toddy?"

"Or bourbon," Dixie added.

"No thanks," Charles said. "Wouldn't happen to have any coffee brewed?"

"Heaven's no," Martha said. "That stuff's not good for you. Let me grab a chair from the kitchen. Wouldn't want you to sit on the floor."

Charles said, "Martha, I'll get it."

She pointed her cane in the direction of the kitchen like Charles wouldn't know how to find it. Fortunately, Dixie was in the chair closest to Squeezy's occupied aquarium, so I sat on the only vacant seat. Charles returned and pulled the kitchen chair up beside Martha.

Martha waited for Charles to get comfortable, then said, "Gentlemen, I appreciate you coming over. I wanted to—"

Dixie interrupted, "Martha, God love her, wanted to be an unvarnished jackass. I told her so in no uncertain terms."

Martha pointed her cane at Dixie. "Dear, why don't you let me explain?"

Yes, Martha, please, I thought.

"It's your house," Dixie said, then took another sip.

"As you recall, when you visited the other day, you asked

if I'd let the young man from Bert's stay here until he found satisfactory housing."

"Ty Striker," Charles said.

"Yes, anyway, I reacted strongly."

"Like a jackass," Dixie added, only to receive a dirty look from her friend.

"I was concerned about how my good friend Dixie and my dearly beloved deceased husband would react to a man moving in with me."

"Cut to the chase, Martha," Dixie said. "You thought we'd think it was for sex."

Martha's face turned red. "Dixie, I don't think that's appropriate talk—"

Again, Dixie interrupted, apparently one of her strengths, "Martha, you know that's what you thought. What did I tell you?"

"Dixie, I don't think—"

"I told you the man from Bert's was young enough to be your grandson, heavens, possibly great-grandson. The last time you had sex that peanut farmer from Georgia was President. I promise sex won't be popping in Ty's head when he sees you. I think it'd be great for you having someone who walks on two legs living in here not slithering around like Squeezy or walking on all fours like most of your family members."

"But, what about—"

"I know, I know. What would Tommy think? I told you he ain't doing a bit of thinking down in that hole in the ground. Not a bit."

Martha leaned forward in her chair, glared at her friend, then said, "Dixie, enough." She turned to Charles, then to me. "Guys, Dixie has some good points. Crudely put, but good. If you think the young man would be interested, I'd be honored for him to move in. As I think you said the last time you were here, this place is too large for me to keep up by myself."

Charles glanced at me. I said, "Martha, I think Ty would be thrilled."

"So would his kitten, Lost," Charles added.

"Martha," I said, "You'll make Ty's Christmas."

"Ladies," Charles said, "will you be at Cal's Christmas party?"

Dixie said, "Can't speak for Martha, but I'll be there. We always go to the potluck supper at Planet Follywood, but that's later."

"Don't know why you can't speak for me, you always do."

"Okay," Dixie said, "Martha will be there. She may even bring her new boy toy." She slapped her knee and laughed. "Then after we get home, he can come-a-courtin' over my way if Martha don't wear him out."

On that, it was time to leave. I told Martha I'd talk to Ty and get back with her.

In the car, I said, "At least we didn't have to put up with any of Martha's animals."

"You got enough dog hair on your butt from the chair to build a dog. I think I would've hugged Squeezy before listening more to Dixie."

"Good point," I said, "as long as it was you holding the boa."

Instead of turning in my drive, Charles drove a hundred feet farther and pulled in Bert's lot.

"Let's tell Ty," Charles said.

Ty was behind the register talking to Shawn, another

friend of mine, holding his tiny dog Bruiser. He was paying for a loaf of bread while Ty was breaking a treat in half and giving it to Bruiser. Shawn left so Charles asked Ty if he had a few minutes. I was no expert, but it appeared Ty was working. I wondered how he'd have time for us. Charles added, "It's important."

A woman stepped behind us with a bag of chips. Ty looked around and asked a man working behind the deli counter if he could cover the register. The man nodded.

Ty said, "Let's go outside. I need to check on Lost."

On the way to his car, I asked if he knew Martha Wright.

"By reputation. Isn't she the woman who feeds strays, has a hundred pets?"

I smiled. "She does feed strays, but her pet count is closer to a dozen."

"Don't think I've talked to her, or if I have, I didn't know who she was. Why?"

I shared that we'd come from her house where she said she'd love for Ty to stay there until he found somewhere more suitable. I explained that Martha's house was on the ocean and had about two-thousand times more living space than his Miata.

"Why would a stranger want to take me in, me in?"

I resisted saying it was because she took in strays. "She knew about the fire, heard you were living in your car, and had Lost. She's an animal lover, so she thought her house would be perfect, that is, if you had any interest."

Yes, some of that was reimagining history, but I wanted it to sound like Martha's idea.

"I'd be thrilled for the opportunity," he said. "When can I meet her?"

I asked when he got off work. He told me six. I told him I'd let her know he'd accept her kind offer, and if okay with her, he could go to her house after work.

"How's that sound?"

"Wonderful."

I gave him Martha's address and Charles gave him her phone number in case he couldn't get there today.

"Oh, one more thing, Mr. Landrum. You were asking me if I knew of anyone who might know about the fire, anyone other than us who lived there."

I vaguely remembered saying something about it. "Yes."

"Did you see that lady behind you in line before we came out here?"

I noticed someone, but that was all. "Yes, why?"

"Today was the first time I've seen her since the fire. It reminded me she talked to me two, maybe three, weeks before the building burned. I was heading to my apartment and she was in the parking lot."

Charles said, "What'd she want?"

"Nothing important. Stuff like how I liked living there, how long I'd been there, if the landlord kept up the building good."

He was right, I didn't see how any of that was important. "Why'd you mention it?"

"I could be wrong, but I think I saw her near the building a time or two after that. Sort of thought it was a little strange, that's all."

"You saw her two or three times before the fire?" I said.

"Think so."

Charles said, "Did she give you her name?"

"Yeah. It was something like Kelsey."

I said, "Could it be Kaycee?"

Ty nodded. "Kaycee, umm. Could be."

I looked back toward the store. A blue SUV was pulling out of the lot, but the windows were tinted. I couldn't see the driver. "Ty, is that her in the blue SUV?"

He looked at the vehicle heading east on Ashley Avenue. "That's her car."

She was driving a Maserati SUV, a blue Maserati like the one parked adjacent to the apartment building's parking lot during the Christmas parade. Of course, there could be more than one blue Maserati SUV on Folly, but what were the odds?

"Ty," I said, "other than asking about the stuff you already mentioned, do you recall her saying anything else?"

He tapped on the Miata's window. Lost jumped from the seat to the headrest then gave Ty a *where's my food* look. Ty opened the door enough to get his hand in and wrapped it around Lost's stomach. The kitten purred as Ty lifted him out of the car, cradling him in the crook of his elbow. Charles being Charles stepped closer to Ty and rubbed Lost under his chin, then told the feline he was getting a new home, a home with animals to play with.

Ty handed Lost to Charles, then turned back to me. "Sorry, Mr. Landrum, what was the question?"

"Do you recall Kaycee saying anything else?"

"Not really. I think she must've been interested in renting an apartment."

Charles continued to rub the underside of his feline friend's chin, but said, "Why think that?"

"She wanted to know if there were vacant units."

He hadn't mentioned that earlier.

I said, "You sure?"

"Yeah. I told her the one on the first floor was empty. I

offered to give her the landlord's name and number. Said she already had it."

Charles handed Lost back to Ty, and said, "Guess that's why she was asking how well he maintained the building."

"That's what I figured."

It could be as simple as that, I thought. Or not.

Charles said, "Did she say anything else?"

"Don't recall anything." He looked at his watch, then slipped Lost back in his car. "Guys, I'd better get back in there. I really need to keep this job."

I thanked him for talking with us and said I'd let Martha know he'd be stopping by after work.

He headed to the store. Charles headed to his car, until I said, "Charles, remember when we were on our way to the fire?"

"Duh, how could I forget? We were on—"

"Let me finish."

He shrugged. "So?"

"Do you remember seeing vehicles in the lot near the apartment building's parking area?"

"Chris, I remember black smoke, red flames, red fire trucks, and two ambulances that nearly ran us down. I don't remember what was parked nearby. Why?"

"One of the vehicles was a blue Maserati SUV."

Charles looked toward Bert's. "Like the one what's her name was driving?"

"Exactly."

"Coincidence?"

"What do you think?"

He continued looking at Bert's like the SUV would return. "Could she live in the building beside the apartment building?"

"No. Cindy told me she lives in a condo near Harris Teeter."

"Think you need to tell Cindy."

I said, "I will."

"I mean now."

I reached for my phone, when Charles added, "Don't forget to push that little speaker icon."

Instead of getting a live voice, Cindy's message informed me she was unable to take the call, for the caller to leave a message. I asked her to call when she got a chance. Charles harrumphed, then mumbled something about where were the police when you needed them.

I told him I'd let him know after I talked to the Chief. He asked if he needed to drive me home so I wouldn't have to walk thirty yards. I said I could manage the voyage. He left me standing in Bert's side parking area.

I was still in the lot when the phone rang. I figured Charles missed hearing Cindy by seconds, but I was wrong. Close, but wrong.

"Chris, this is Rose, Cindy's sister. Did I catch you at a bad time?"

I said no and resisted asking her if she could teach my friends phone etiquette.

"I'm calling as Luke's social secretary," she said then chuckled. "We're heading to Planet Follywood in a few minutes for lunch. Luke said how much you liked the restaurant. He wanted me to call to see if you'd join us."

I said I'd be honored. I also realized this was the first time in my adult life a pre-teen had his social secretary call to invite me to share a meal.

Chapter Thirty-Four

I approached Luke and Rose's table.

"Mr. Landrum," Luke said, "You said you loved eating here, so I asked mom to call you."

I thanked him for the invitation as a server arrived and put a glass of what appeared to be iced tea in front of Rose, a soft drink beside Luke. He asked if I wanted anything. I said water was fine.

"Luke," I said, "did Uncle Larry give you the day off?"

"No, he said with Christmas two days away, he needed all the help he could get. I told him even a little boy has to eat. He said I could bring mom here for lunch."

"You're a tough negotiator," I said.

He smiled like I'd called him king of the world.

"This is part of my Christmas gift," Rose said. "Luke is using his own money to buy lunch."

"Mr. Landrum, because you've been so nice to me, I want to buy yours too."

The phone rang before I told him that wasn't necessary. Bob Howard's name appeared on the screen.

"Hi, Bob."

"Aren't you going to insult me like you usually do?"

"It's Christmas, besides, you have that backward."

"Whatever. I have el scoopo on that woman you asked about."

"Hang on a second," I said, then told my lunch mates I needed to take the call then headed to the back of the restaurant.

"Okay," I said.

"If that was a second, you need a better watch. Ready for el scoopo?"

"Ready."

"Kaycee Ericson. Late-forties, good looking according to the old coots I talked to. She divorced Alan Ericson a while back. Alan is a big-time developer in Charleston, but he's done projects as far away as Asheville. Mostly large apartment complexes. Anyway, his ex took a bunch of money in the divorce. She built a small office building a half-block off Center Street in your town, and either two or three oceanfront McMansions. My source was vague on the number. As even you, as ignorant as you are about anything building wise, know, your zoning regulators are doing everything they can to limit new construction, especially super-sized buildings on property that originally held small beach houses. In other words, Kaycee has been running into brick walls instead of open arms from those in control."

I'd heard something similar from Cindy and shared that with Bob.

"Okay, know it all, did you hear she's trying to find

properties, mostly multi-unit properties where the owners are, let's say, having financial difficulties?"

"That's new."

"Like all good storytellers, I saved the best for last."

I waited for him to continue, he didn't, so I assumed he wanted me to beg for the best. "What's that, Mr. Fount of Information?"

"That's better. One of my sources said several years ago, one of Alan Ericson's apartment buildings had a horrible fire. Was it caused by lightning? No. Electrical problem? No. How about by Aunt Sally leaving something on the stove? Nope, again. Now that I've given you all the clues, think you can guess the cause?"

"Arson?"

"You're smarter than the average cucumber. There was a ton of speculation that Alan set the fire, but not an ounce of proof."

"You're saying that Kaycee is guilty by marriage?"

"Nope. I'm telling you what happened. You figure out the rest."

"Anything else?"

"Hell, do I have to get you a signed, notarized confession?"

"If you don't mind."

He must've minded. He hung up.

That didn't prove Kaycee started the fire but was information Cindy needed. Seeing Luke staring in my direction, it'd have to wait.

I returned to the table and Luke's broad smile.

"Mr. Landrum, I made an executive decision, although mom said I shouldn't."

"What was that, Luke?"

"I ordered your lunch. I got you the same thing you had when we were here the last time. I figured you liked it, or you wouldn't have got it then."

"Excellent decision, Luke."

His smile increased. "See Mom, told you so."

"Everything okay?" Rose said, then nodded her head in the direction where I'd been.

"Yes. Is your sister working today? I left her a message earlier but haven't heard from her."

"As far as I know. She said she had several meetings."

Luke interrupted, "Aunt Cindy said yucky meetings."

"Luke, you know not to interrupt," Rose said.

He bowed his head.

Rose turned to me. "You haven't heard from her today?"

"No, why?"

"Last night, she told me she had news about the fire. She was going to call you."

Lunch arrived. I wasn't the only one to order the same meal as last time. A hot dog was placed in front of Luke, a cheeseburger for Rose, and my chicken fingers. As much as I wanted to fight it, most of us are creatures of habit. We ate silently for a couple of minutes, but I kept going back to what Ty and Bob had said.

"Rose, this may be a strange question, but do you remember seeing a blue Maserati SUV parked near the apartment complex?"

"I don't pay much attention to cars, never have."

Luke said, "I do."

Rose said, "Luke's best friend's dad owns a Chevy dealership in Morristown."

"Len's dad is cool," Luke said. "He lets us roam around the lot. When the repair shop is closed, we can go in there.

His dad says insurance wouldn't let us go in when mechanics are working."

That got my attention, about paying attention, not about his friend Len. "Do you mean you pay attention to cars, or do you remember seeing a blue SUV?"

Rose patted her son on the arm. "See, Luke, how you say things is important."

He sighed, "I know, mom. You tell me all the time."

I can't imagine how it would be growing up with an English teacher mom.

I said. "Luke, help me understand what you mean."

He glanced at Rose then turned to me. "It's sort of both, Mr. Landrum. I like looking at cars, especially new ones. And, I remember seeing a blue Maserati."

"Do you remember when you saw it?"

"Day after we moved in. I thought it was cool looking. I hadn't seen one."

"Was that the only time you saw it?"

"Umm, two more times, I think."

"When?"

"Suppose the next time was the day before the fire. It was close to our lot. Then I saw it the morning we were walking to watch the Christmas parade."

"Where was it?"

"Parked at the road. I figured the lady in it was going to move in our building."

"Why?"

"Mom and me were walking up our street when—"

"Mom and I, Luke," Rose said.

Luke made a noise that sounded like a braying horse. I bit the inside of my lip to keep from laughing.

"Yes, mom." He continued, "Mom and I were headed

toward the street where the parade was going to be. I looked back and saw the lady carrying a large box, sort of like those boxes we packed stuff in to move here. I figured she was moving in."

"Luke, are you sure she came out of the blue SUV?"

Rose looked at Luke, then at me with narrowed eyes.

"Yes, sir. Know it was her. She didn't move in, did she? Someone said the next-door apartment was still empty when the fire started."

I ate the chicken fingers, but they could easily have been glued sawdust for all the attention I paid to them. I held my need to talk to Cindy in check and tried to make Luke's lunch for his mom and me as positive as possible.

I must not have shown as much anxiety as I felt. We finished and Luke said it'd been a wonderful Christmas lunch, that we ought to do it again.

All I wanted to do again was talk to Chief LaMond. She may be convinced that Russell O'Leary torched his building. I thought I had a persuasive argument she was wrong.

Chapter Thirty-Five

Instead of going home after lunch, I crossed Center Street and headed toward the combination City Hall and Department of Public Safety building. Cindy's pickup wasn't in the lot behind the building, so I changed direction to head home.

Patience may be a virtue, but with me, it's often in short supply. I was tempted to leave the Chief another message but knew she'd call when she got a chance. By five-thirty, my head was about to explode from waiting.

Fortunately, it didn't, so I was able to answer the phone. It was Cindy.

"Thank goodness you called," I said. "I've learned—"

"Hold that thought. Meet me at the Surf Bar in fifteen minutes. A day of meetings, boring meetings, and a trip downtown with the mayor, have me needing a cold beer more than anything you have to say."

The Surf Bar was across the street from the entrance to the Public Safety building, making it convenient for Cindy when she needed to escape her office. I got there in ten minutes to find her at a table near the door, gripping a beer in a Terrapin Beer Company glass. The turtle in the logo looked happier than the Chief.

"Rough day?" I said as I sat across from her at the small table.

"Spent most of it battling two councilmembers who think I'm spending too much money on overtime, one councilmember who thinks I need to increase police presence near his house, of course, then two hours in the car with our mayor listening to three million things he thinks the police need to do better. How do you think my day was?"

"You've had better."

"I've had better days at the dentist when she forgot to give me enough numbing juice before jackhammering on a molar. With griping out of the way, there is a bright side and a bad side."

"I suppose you're going to tell me both."

Cindy looked at the ceiling where dollar bills were attached to most non-moving surfaces. White Christmas lights were strung from the columns and roof trusses. I call them Christmas lights because that was their original purpose, but they're year-round fixtures in the Surf Bar.

"Chris, that's the least I can do since you're buying me this, and another, and another."

"It's my pleasure," I said with a tinge of sarcasm.

"Russell O'Leary," she said like that explained everything. "I had a nice long conversation with him this morning before every elected official in our fair city tried to take a chunk of my hide."

I've known the bartender for a few years, so he had a server bring me a glass of red wine without me having to say anything. That's one good thing about living in a small town. I took a sip, while Cindy stared at me.

I said, "What?"

"I'm waiting for your full attention. This is a fun-filled story."

"Proceed."

"Landlord Russell lied about where he was and why?"

"Is that the bright side?"

"Is for him. Seems he has a heart condition, some long Latin word I couldn't define, pronounce, or spell. Suffice to say, it's serious. His Charleston cardiologist referred him to some world-renowned specialist at the Emory University Hospital near Atlanta, the keyword being near, as opposed to being in downtown Atlanta. Russell didn't want his employer to know about the condition. He especially didn't want his wife and kids to know. Didn't want them to worry, he claimed." She took a sip of beer, shook her head, then continued. "He made up the whole story about being at a get-rich-quick seminar."

"Why'd he lie to you? Did he think you'd tell his employer or his wife?"

"Chris, in my entire life, I've never been a man. Most of the time, I don't know how you dudes think. Hell, I know how you act, but not think. Assuming you think. I don't know why he decided to stick me with the feeble story. He's still above ground, so I assume it worked with his wife."

"What did the Emory doctor say?"

"Said he has a heart. Whatever is wrong with it can be fixed with some expensive meds, or that's what Russell said. Since he's a proven liar, I don't know if I believe it. What I am certain is he was in Georgia when his building went up in smoke. He showed me a hotel bill, two gas receipts, and a food receipt from a Waffle House." She shook her head. "Who in the hell keeps Waffle House receipts?"

"You're a female, you wouldn't understand," I joked, or thought it was a joke.

Cindy didn't laugh, didn't smile, didn't say anything. Women often don't appreciate how witty men are.

"Chief, if that's the good side, what's the bad side?"

"I'm sitting here, feeling sorry for myself, without anyone to nominate for arsonist of the year."

I took a sip, smiled, then said, "Let me see if I can help. Did you get a chance to talk to Kaycee Ericson?"

"Not yet. Been wasting my time trying to prove Russell did something far worse than lie to his wife and me. Why? No, don't answer that. Did she start the fire? Do you have proof?"

"Proof, no, but let me tell you what I've learned."

She finished the beer and raised her glass for the server to bring a refill. "I'm all ears."

"I was talking with Ty who told me Kaycee approached him at the apartment building days before the fire. Started asking questions like how long he'd lived there, was the building well maintained, etc."

"What got Ty talking about that?"

"Charles and I went to Bert's to tell him that Martha Wright said he could stay at her place until he found somewhere else to live."

"Whoa, how'd that come about?"

I told her the story about approaching Martha a few days ago, her rejection of the idea, and why.

"Cindy almost choked on her beer, cleared her throat, then said, "Martha, the woman who's about two hundred years old, thought her neighbor would think she was a cougar? Crapola, I thought I'd heard it all."

I didn't add what Martha said her deceased husband would think. Instead, I told her about Martha's change of heart.

"That's great, but what does it have to do with Kaycee?"

"Nothing other than it's the reason Charles and I were talking to Ty."

"Charles was with you?"

I nodded.

"Figures. Okay, go ahead with something I'd be interested in."

"Kaycee asked Ty about vacant units. He thought she may want to rent one."

"More interesting. Like the vacant unit where the fire started?"

"That's the one. Ty also told us she was driving a blue Maserati SUV. He pointed it out in Bert's lot."

"That's important, how?"

"When Charles and I were walking up Ashley Avenue on our way to see what was burning, I saw a blue Maserati SUV in that small lot beside the apartment's parking area. Didn't you tell me Kaycee lives out by Harris Teeter?"

Cindy nodded.

"So, I wondered why her car, okay maybe not hers, but isn't it unlikely there're two blue Maserati SUVs over here?"

"I've never seen one. So, it's rare but not impossible. Go on."

I told her what Bob Howard's research uncovered, with emphasis on how Kaycee's ex-husband had been a suspect in an arson. I took a sip of wine, then added, "Do you know who I had lunch with today?"

"Dolly Parton?"

"Guess again."

"I'm guessed out. Who?"

"Your sister and nephew. Luke said he had so much fun eating with me last week, he had his mom invite me today."

"That boy needs to get out more and meet some fun people. How did Larry let him escape from the store?"

I laughed. "Luke said he told Larry that employees need to eat."

"Smart kid. I suppose there's a reason you're telling me this."

"Yes, a good one." I then bullet-pointed the highlights of our discussion.

"Are you telling me Luke saw Kaycee carrying a box to the apartment building less than an hour before the fire?"

"That's what I'm telling you."

"Let me wrap this around my undersized brain. I had the most significant clue to who started the fire living under my roof."

I nodded.

"Crap, I should kick myself in the butt and turn in my badge."

I didn't ask how she planned to do the first part of that. Instead, I said, "Cindy, you couldn't have known. It only came up because I asked Luke about the blue SUV."

She lowered her head and stared in her beer. "Yet an old geezer with no law enforcement training figures it out."

I smiled. "Yeah, but Charles is teaching me all the tricks of being a detective."

She let out a string of profanities, none of which bear repeating.

I waited for her blood pressure to lower to non-stroke

levels, then said, "It's a lot of circumstantial evidence, but what are the chances of getting a conviction on what you now know?"

"Slim, but it gives me a lot more to talk about tomorrow when I pay a Christmas Eve visit to Ms. Ericson."

"Excellent plan," I said, then told her I had to get home to wait for Neil Wilson, my new housemate, to arrive.

"You letting someone stay at your place. Will Christmas miracles never cease?"

Chapter Thirty-Six

Christmas Eve began with me sleeping late combined with rumbles of snores coming from my former office, current guest bedroom. It took a minute to remember why the snoring wasn't in my dreams but from my new houseguest. Neil had arrived last night, thanked me just under five hundred times for letting him stay, then adjusted to his new environment. He knew from working at Cal's I wasn't a beer drinker, so he brought a six-pack with him. Three cans were in the refrigerator this morning. He'd shared he often worked late, so I shouldn't expect to see him much in the mornings. I thought that was great since I'm a morning person who enjoys peace and quiet. I hadn't contemplated snoring.

I turned on the Mr. Coffee machine, then headed to Bert's for a box of donuts, and a chance to ask Ty about his move to Martha's. Ty wasn't at his usual hangout behind the register, so I asked if he was working. Denise, another of

Bert's uber-helpful employees said he wasn't coming in until noon.

When I got home, Neil was at the kitchen table, wearing orange and green flannel pajamas, and staring in one of my red I Love Folly Beach mugs. He continued staring in the mug, and said, "Did you know there's nothing to eat in your kitchen?"

I dropped the box of donuts on the table. "Bon Appetit."

I think he smiled, although it looked more like a frown.

"Sleep well?" I asked instead of telling him there was never food in the kitchen.

He opened the donuts, took a bite, then mumbled, "Think so."

Fifteen minutes later, with food in his stomach, caffeine in his veins, Neil reentered the world of the living with full sentences and stories about some of last night's more memorable customers. I suspected much of his conversation was from nervous energy rather than wanting me to know what each customer ordered, or what they were doing Christmas.

Ten o'clock rolled around quicker than it does with me here alone. I was wondering if Cindy had caught up with Kaycee Ericson. By eleven, I was tempted to call the Chief. Remember, patience isn't one of my virtues.

I didn't have to show the Chief my lack of patience. My phone rang at eleven fifteen revealing her name on the screen.

She began with, "Is this the Chris Landrum homeless shelter?"

"What'd you learn, Cindy?"

Okay, she was reminded of my lack of patience.

"Chill, it's Christmas Eve. Tis the season to be jolly."

I said, "Ho, Ho, Ho. What'd you learn?"

"You're no fun. Okay, at oh-nine-hundred this morning, I knocked on Kaycee's condo door. At nine-hundred one, nine-hundred two, nine-hundred three I knocked, all to no avail. Additionally, there wasn't a Maserati SUV in the lot. I used all my chiefly skills to deduce she wasn't home."

"What now?"

"Glad you asked. This is where it gets interesting. I returned to my majestic office and used my chiefly skills to access my secret, super-duper databases to check on Kaycee's said condo. Want to guess what I found?"

"It's too early for guessing."

"You wouldn't get it anyway. It seems the condo isn't owned by Kaycee but belongs to one Anthony Craft, a resident of Coral Gables, Florida. I called Mr. Craft, a call answered by his wife Madeline, who, once I assured her I wasn't Anthony's mistress, handed the phone to her hubby. I identified myself. then after explaining there wasn't anything wrong with his rental unit, he calmed down."

There was a long pause, so I said, "You still there?"

"Cool your jets. I'm looking for the rest of my notes. Got them. Okay, Anthony rented his condo to Kaycee two years ago. She occasionally was late on rent, but always paid, didn't complain about anything, and according to Anthony, was perfect for his condo, whatever that meant."

"I don't suppose he mentioned that she was an arsonist?"

"No, but know what he did share?"

"What?"

"His tenant called two days ago saying she was moving. Her lease expires the end of the month and she wouldn't be renewing. Anthony was saddened since she'd been such a good tenant, in other words, all he had to do was sit in beautiful Florida and cash rent checks."

"Did he say where she was going?"

"Nope. That would've been too easy. She said something about going back up north, which could be New England, Canada, the North Pole."

"What now?"

"I'm going to pick you up in ten minutes and we're going to make another visit to Anthony's condo."

"I thought you determined no one was there?"

"There isn't, but helpful Anthony gave me the keypad lock combination, plus the lawyerly super-important authorization to inspect the unit."

Cindy was out front blowing her horn five minutes later. Five minutes after that, we were standing in front of Kaycee's condo, with Cindy punching numbers on the keypad. She asked me to stand back as she entered. Not seeing anything amiss, or Kaycee pointing a gun at her, Cindy invited me in, reminding me not to touch anything.

The large, open floor plan unit was painted a cheery off-yellow with typical condo-package furniture. I didn't see anything indicating it'd been inhabited. There were no knickknacks or photos on the tables, no newspapers, magazines, or brochures setting around. Cindy took a quick scan around the room then went into the kitchen. I followed her and noticed a dirty plate, a butter knife, and three glasses in the sink. The Chief pulled out a tall trash container from under the counter. A used coffee filter, coffee grounds, and three pieces of paper torn in half were all the container held.

I followed Cindy down a narrow hall to the first

bedroom. It looked like it'd never been used. A colorful bedspread was untouched, the pillow looked like it'd just come from the store. The closet was empty. The second bedroom didn't look any more used than the first.

The master bedroom was another story. The bedspread lay on the floor, the sheets mussed, the pillow dented where a head would've rested. Several hangers were strewn across the bed, two more on the floor, the closet door stood open, with more hangers on the rod. All were empty.

I was searching the corners of the closet, then looking under the bed, hoping to find anything indicating Kaycee was the arsonist. Cindy had begun pulling out dresser drawers.

She said, "Huh?"

"What?"

She pointed at two books she'd found in the bottom drawer. One was about buying real estate in both good and bad markets, the other on creative financing options. She was flipping through a copy-paper sized Office Depot wire-bound notebook.

"Where was that?"

"Under the books."

I moved closer to see what Cindy was seeing. Part of the first page had been ripped out. There were sketches on the next three pages. They looked like draft floor plans. What really got my attention was the paper, more accurately, graph paper.

"Cindy, remember I told you about the note under Noelle's windshield?"

"Politely telling her to get off Folly or no telling what?"

"That's the one."

"So what?"

"It was on graph paper."

"You didn't tell me that."

"Didn't think it was important."

"Bet you do now."

She didn't give me a chance to answer. She continued, "You said the note burned in the fire?"

I nodded.

She sighed. "More circumstantial evidence."

I took my phone out of my pocket and tapped in Noelle's number. She answered on the second ring.

"Noelle, this is Chris. Where are you?"

"Barb's Books, why?"

"If you're going to be there a few minutes, I'd like talk to you."

She said she'd wait. I hung up and turned to Cindy. "Let's visit Noelle."

"Why? The note's gone."

"I have an idea."

Cindy was kind not to push. "Okay."

"Take the notepad."

"Don't suppose you're going to tell me why?"

"Not yet."

Barb was behind the counter running a credit card through the machine then bagging three books.

She saw Cindy and me, pointed to the backroom, and said Noelle was waiting for us.

Noelle was pacing the small room. She wore a gray sweatshirt, jeans, and of course, sunglasses. She smiled when she saw me, the look turned inquisitive when she noticed the Chief behind me.

"Thanks for waiting. Have a seat."

She slowly lowered herself in the chair behind Barb's chrome and glass desk. "Is everything okay?"

"Yes," I said then pulled a chair up to the side of the desk. Cindy remained standing as I removed a sheet of copy paper from the printer.

"Noelle, didn't you tell me the note you found under your windshield was on paper that looked like it'd been torn from a larger sheet?"

She looked at Cindy, then her gaze turned to me. "Umm, yes. Why?"

"Noelle, this may seem silly, but bear with me." I handed her the piece of copy paper off Barb's printer. "Tear this about the size of the note you found."

"Chris, I don't remember exactly how big it was."

"I understand, give it your best shot."

She took the paper, began to rip it in half, stopped, then tore it about an inch lower than where she first started. She handed me the piece that was about one-third of the paper I'd handed her.

Cindy must've figured out what I was doing. She flipped open the pad she'd brought with her and set it on the desk. I took the piece Noelle had given me and laid it on the open pad. It wasn't a perfect match for what had been torn out of the pad, but close.

Noelle who hadn't said anything since she handed me the torn sheet, touched the pad, looked at Cindy, at me, then said, "Graph paper."

"Like the note you got," I added.

"Exactly."

Chapter Thirty-Seven

Christmas began with a call from Cindy wishing me Merry Christmas, then telling me there was an APB out on Kaycee Ericson's SUV. She hadn't been found, but she'd used her credit card to buy gas at an Interstate station in Lumberton, North Carolina, and later near Richmond, Virginia. She may not have been caught, but was heading away, far away, from Folly Beach, South Carolina. For that I was thankful.

I was then surprised when Neil stepped in the kitchen and handed me a bottle of Cabernet with a red ribbon tied around it.

My housemate said, "Merry Christmas."

I was touched. "Neil, you didn't have to do that. I didn't get you anything."

"Chris, hush. You gave me the best gift I could ever get. You gave me a place to stay and knowing someone cared enough to make it available."

I thanked him then asked what he was doing up so early.

"Cal's so excited about his party, he wants me to come early to help get everything ready. I've never seen that old boy so amped."

"Christmas is his biggest day of the year." I told Neil about why having the party meant so much to the country crooner.

"I'll do whatever I can to make sure it's a success. Saying that, I'd better get dressed and over there. I'll grab something at Bert's community Christmas breakfast, so you won't have to fix anything fancy." He laughed at his joke, patted me on the back, then said he'd see me at the party.

Cal's Christmas gala was scheduled to begin at one o'clock, but the allure of free food and drink always brought attendees before the official opening. I wanted to be there early in case I could help.

I walked through the door surrounded by colorful lights at twelve-thirty. The room was already half full. Brenda Lee's "Rockin' Around the Christmas Tree" was playing, along with laughter coming from people at a table in the center of the room holding three bowls of salsa, avocado dip, and a basket of chips large enough to hold a beach-ball. Always early Charles was talking with Dude Sloan cradling Pluto in his arms. Dogs aren't allowed in Cal's, but it was Christmas. Besides, a good argument could be made Dude needed a service animal. I don't know what was said, but Charles was laughing louder than I'd heard in months.

All four trees were glowing brightly as were the countless strands of Christmas lights throughout the room. Cal was standing behind the bar pulling a beer out of the cooler. The LED lights on his Stetson blinked, his red polo shirt was so bright I suspected it'd glow in the dark. His smile was priceless. Neil was at the other end of the bar fiddling with a stack of red napkins.

Two men I didn't know arrived next. They waved at Cal who returned the wave then pointed toward the chips. They filled a paper plate with chips and headed to the bar where Cal shook their hands and offered each a drink. They didn't hesitate taking the drinks. Kristin, a part-time server who'd worked at Cal's for several years, and Joy, another server who'd joined Cal's a year ago, were moving a couple of tables around so there was more room for people to stand.

Burl arrived wearing a Santa hat and the sweater he wore to last year's party. It was easy to remember since it could win any ugly Christmas sweater contest.

"Merry Christmas, Brother Chris."

"The same to you, Preacher. Glad to see you. I know Cal will be happy you're here."

"Hope he's not happy enough to drag me on stage."

"Preacher, it's a Christmas tradition."

"Like grandpa getting drunk on eggnog," Burl said, then smiled.

Charles left Dude and Pluto talking with someone I didn't know and headed to the bar, where he said something to Neil, then grabbed a couple of drinks from the cooler. He handed the drinks to two men who were leaning against the bar. I smiled, knowing how much Charles loves helping others. He was in his element.

Gene Autry's version of "Here Comes Santa Claus" interrupted Burl's bemoaning the Christmas tradition. He said he'd better say hi to the host and left me standing near the front door enjoying the festive environment. I didn't see Martha Wright until she tapped me with her cane. She had a gleam in her eyes, either for being able to celebrate

Christmas at Cal's or from Christmas morning hot toddies. Dixie was behind her. Each wore red Christmas sweaters; neither sweater could compete with Burl's for tackiness.

Dixie stepped in front of her neighbor. "Martha tells me this is one whale of a party."

Martha had attended for the first-time last year.

"She's right," I said. "Is Ty with you?"

"That boy's a gem," Martha said. "He was up at the crack of dawn. Fed my kids, fixed toast to go with my oatmeal, and," she chuckled. "Fixed me a hot toddy. Then he went to work for a few hours. Did I mention he was a gem?"

Yes, but didn't remind her. I didn't catch the answer to my question, so I repeated, "Is he here?"

"He's parking my car. I let him chauffeur us in the Lincoln. Told him he didn't even have to wear one of those chauffeur hats." She looked over my shoulder. "Heavens, here he is."

"Merry Christmas, Mr. Landrum," Ty said as we shook hands.

"Martha," Dixie said, "are we going to stand here and yak all day or we going to the bar?"

I had the impression she'd already found one. Martha put her arm around her neighbor and pulled her toward the drinks. Ty shrugged and followed the women. Three more people, two women and a man, I knew to be regulars entered and headed to the food.

Noelle, closely followed by Barb, stepped through the entry and looked around. Barb saw me and motioned for Noelle to join her as she gave me a hug and a kiss. I looked up to see if there was mistletoe. There wasn't. Noelle gave me a tentative hug. Both ladies wore red blouses and black slacks. I suspected Noelle's blouse came from Barb's closet.

We weaved our way through a group of people on our way to the salsa table, as Barb said, "Noelle told me about what you wanted with her in the store yesterday. Has Cindy found Kaycee?"

We got plates of food, Noelle went to thank Cal for hosting the party, and Barb and I moved to a corner of the room.

I told her Kaycee hadn't been caught, but she was several states away and traveling away from Folly.

"Good, Noelle was so worried, thinking she should have done something different when she got the note."

"I doubt it would've helped, besides what she told Cindy about the paper will be a big help."

"That's what I told her. Any idea why Kaycee set the fire?"

"The theory is so she could buy the lot from Russell O'Leary. He'd originally said he'd sell to her, then his kids and wife convinced him to keep it for their future. Kaycee probably figured he'd have no need for it if it was reduced to ashes."

"Putting on my lawyer's hat, they could probably get a conviction based on a decent amount of circumstantial evidence, especially the note. I'm still confused about why Kaycee wrote the note only to Noelle. If she was going to burn the building, and not harm anyone, why not warn everyone?"

"I suspect it had to do with Noelle spying on everyone around town while getting ideas for her novel. She could've seen Kaycee near the building. Kaycee could also have seen her and figured she was a loose end she needed to scare off before starting the fire."

"Makes sense."

"Know what makes more sense?"

"What?"

"Getting a drink, some food, and enjoying Cal's party."

We were on our way to the bar when I saw Rose, Luke, and Cindy at the door. Rose and Cindy were in red sweat-shirts, Luke had on a white and red T-shirt. All wore huge smiles. With their entry, there was more red in here than at a University of Georgia football game.

Luke ran over, motioned me to lean down, and whispered, "Mom and Aunt Cindy love the shark jewelry. Thank you for helping me with it."

I told him it was my pleasure, took his hand, and walked him to the bar.

"Cal, you have a special drink back there for my young friend?"

"How about a root beer, partner?" Cal said and tipped his Stetson to Luke.

Luke laughed. "You're funny."

Cal fixed him his drink then he headed back to Rose.

Cindy had her phone to her ear, nodded, then headed out the door. I started to follow, but figured it was none of my business. She returned with a big smile on her face and motioned me over.

"Chris, guess who's spending Christmas day in the hoosegow in Hartford, Connecticut?"

"Our favorite arsonist?"

Her smile widened. "Yep."

"Sorry she's missing Cal's party, aren't you?"

"Nope."

"Me either."

"I'd better go tell my baby sister."

She headed toward Rose, and I moved closer to Noelle who was still standing beside Cal. She said, "Cal, this is my first time in here. I think I need to add a bar like this in my novel. Add a character like you."

Cal tipped his hat, this time at Noelle. "Darlin', I'm a whole novel all by myself."

Noelle laughed. No truer words had ever been spoken.

Cal excused himself, saying he had to say a word or two to the group that now was filling the room, with more arriving.

Fifteen minutes later, Cal tapped on the antique silver microphone in the center of the low stage, then said, "How about lending me an ear?" It took a second tap on the mic before Cal had everyone's attention. "Guys and gals, Merry Christmas. This here's our biggest Christmas shindig ever. Now let me tell from the get-go, I'm not going to be happy unless all of you are. We've all got a bunch to be thankful for, so let's celebrate it. After you eat and drink a bunch more, me and Preacher Burl will be entertaining you with a Christmas duet."

I saw Luke tug on his mom's shirt and whisper something to her, probably, "Cal should've said, Preacher and I, not me and Preacher." Rose smiled and fluffed his hair.

Janice Raque was standing in the doorway, looking around. I left the bar to meet her. Before I could make it through the crowd, Preacher Burl was talking with her. She looked toward the ceiling, then hugged Burl before I could reach the two.

Janice turned to me. "Chris, you'll never guess what Preacher Burl told me."

"What?"

"Someone moved out of Hope House yesterday after-noon. The preacher said I could have the room if I wanted it. You bet your as—umm, you bet I do."

Burl smiled. "Brother Chris, I told you I had faith it'd work out."

"That you did, Preacher."

Hank Williams Sr was finishing his classic version of "I Saw the Light" when Cal pulled the plug on the jukebox, stepped behind the silver mic, and said, "Y'all ready for it?" He cupped his hand behind his ear.

A few celebrators took the hint. "Yes."

"Preacher, get your holy body up here."

Burl was standing beside me and I was afraid he was going to bolt for the door. In the spirit of Christmas, he didn't. He sighed as he slowly made his way to the stage. Cal slung his guitar over his head, whispered something to Burl, then pushed the preacher close to the mic. Cal played two chords, nudged Burl's head closer to the mic, then sang:

"O Come, all ye faithful,

Joyful and triumphant,

O come ye, O come ye, to Bethlehem…."

About the Author

Bill Noel is the best-selling author of eighteen novels in the popular Folly Beach Mystery series. Besides being an award-winning novelist, Noel is a fine arts photographer and lives in Louisville, Kentucky, with his wife, Susan, and his off-kilter imagination. Learn more about the series, and the author by visiting www.billnoel.com.